Despo Pavlou is a debut author who has recently completed her first manuscript. She is the older of two, born to Greek Cypriot parents, who immigrated to South Africa in the 1960s. Despo has a strong entrepreneurial spirit and has owned and managed her businesses for 30 years. She spends her time focusing on her new found love, writing and travelling between Cyprus and South Africa to be with her mother, brother and her four adult children.

To my parents, Ioannis and Stavroulla, for loving me through it all.

To my brother Gabriel who's always got my back.

To my four children Vinnie, Giovanni, Rebecca and Stavro, who make this life so epic and have shared my excitement on this journey of my first manuscript. Living life with you is an absolute blast. I'm having fun.

Despo Pavlou

MY KIND OF NORMAL

AUSTIN MACAULEY PUBLISHERS™

LONDON • CAMBRIDGE • NEW YORK • SHARJAH

A CIP catalogue record for this title is available from the British Library.

ISBN 9781398479531 (Paperback)
ISBN 9781398479548 (ePub e-book)

www.austinmacauley.com

First Published 2023
Austin Macauley Publishers Ltd®
1 Canada Square
Canary Wharf
London
E14 5AA

Thanks to Austin Macauley Publishers for saying yes and putting such effort into making it a success.

Table of Contents

Love Is Love   **13**

Chapter 1: Valentines   15

Chapter 2: Irene   17

Chapter 3: Mario   21

Chapter 4: Stefano (Stef)   27

Chapter 5: Boy or Girl   29

Chapter 6: Andrea   31

Chapter 7: Sofia   33

Chapter 8: Dimitri   35

Chapter 9: The End   37

Chapter 10: Sarah   38

Chapter 11: Cyprus   43

Chapter 12: Emma (Em)   47

Chapter 13: Fear   50

Chapter 14: The Dream for Em   57

Chapter 15: New Home, New Life   62

Chapter 16: The Crack in the Armour   64

Chapter 17: Holly   69

Chapter 18: The Envelope   72

Chapter 19: The Broken Promise   78

Chapter 20: Em's Disappointment   81

Chapter 21: Help   84

Chapter 22: Celine   86

Chapter 23: The Call, "HI, Irene"   89

Chapter 24: Relief   94

Chapter 25: Em's New Home   96

Chapter 26: Flirting   99

Chapter 27: Theresa   106

Chapter 28: Check Mate   114

Chapter 29: You Had Me at Hello   118

Chapter 30: Long Distance   124

Chapter 31: Ma   127

Chapter 32; The Accident   131

Chapter 33: The Move   138

Chapter 34: The Business   140

Chapter 35: The Party   144

Chapter 36: Dear Diary   146

Chapter 37: The Aftermath   151

Chapter 38: Cars for Emma   154

Chapter 39: The Realisation 157

Chapter 40: The Talk 161

Chapter 41: Therapy 165

Chapter 42: Reunited 167

Chapter 43: Lets Let Go 170

Chapter 44: Our Home 172

Chapter 45: The Legal Work 174

Chapter 46: The Recovery 176

Chapter 47: Hope 178

Love Is Love

Chapter 1
Valentines

Oh God…not again, I thought.

14 February – Valentine's Day and we thought it would be a nice idea to attend the local Valentine's party. Maybe to encourage romance, maybe to fix everything in our relationship, or maybe just to kill some time on a Saturday evening. We weren't sure, but we were trying, and trying means trying so here we are. Hand in hand because that's what you do when you're trying. You hold hands, you chat, pretend to care about the millionth opinion he's offered that day to make the world a 'functional' place, maybe dance but not really because he doesn't like dancing.

We sit around a well decorated table with six other people who work at the local pub. Mostly acquaintances, not friends. To be fair, we didn't have much time for friends and the last friend I had, I fell in love with.

"Irene, Mario, meet Emma and Derek." I look up and…Oh God…not again. She's stunning. I'm sure it's evident all over my face because I refuse to look away from her. I try, but it doesn't happen. *Say something*, I think as I hear the distant murmurs of "nice to meet you". I reach for her hand and realise that's the hand I want to actually hold. I force my stare away from hers and turn to Derek who is handsome and huge. The tallest man I have ever seen. They're both so happy and lively having just come off the dance floor.

"I hope this town will be good to you," I hear the words slip out my mouth as I excitedly glanced back at her. My soul comes to life, my heart's not sure it can do this again. It almost killed me the last time. Please guard yourself, I hear my pleading heart pounding in my throat. The table number jumps to ten. They're sitting with us.

"That's the biggest man I've ever seen in my life," I whisper to Mario.

"He's not that big," barks Mario in my ear.

We hit it off. Of course we do. Why would it be simple? Why could she not be a big bore so that actually I never have to feel the urge to stare at her and hang onto every little word that slips out of her perfectly formed mouth? He's an accountant, she's an attorney. Most of the conversation that night revolves entirely around Emma. That's who I want to know all about after all. Music is a faint interference in the background until Shania Twain's *Man I Feel Like a Woman* starts playing. She jumps up, looks at me and asks me to dance. Excitedly I jump up, look at Mario to make it look less suspicious and say, "Let's go," hoping this is not the time he decides dancing is a good thing to try. He declines and the energy on the dance floor is tantalising. Everybody sitting at that table knows I loved a woman, my friend, my partner, my all for a year. The very year before this last one. They all see what's happening again but everyone is polite enough to not say anything. Well, not say anything for a few days anyway.

Chapter 2
Irene

I was born and raised in the beautiful port city of Cape Town, a thriving city which favoured business, farming and industry. Cape Town is situated in the South Western pointof South Africa in the Western Cape Province and is South Africa's oldest city, serving as the country's legislative capital. I was born the oldest and only daughter to Paul and Helen and five years after my birth, my parents were blessed with a gorgeous little boy, Ioannis. Despite Ma yearning for a third child, doctors advised her that there would be complications that could lead to the loss of her life and so she tucked her dream of a third child away. John, as he was affectionately known, survived his childhood with me, as I was so often told. He survived the push down the stairs incident, the shoving of peri-peri cashew nuts down his throat and my personal favourite because it resulted in him breaking his arm twice, was using him as a human aeroplaneas I sent him into the wall, to see how high he could fly from take-off point, my legs. John and I were raised in a traditional Greek home – raised on good food, great love and the Greek Orthodox Church. We all know what Orthodox means, do we not?

We grew up in a tight-knit Greek community and even though it was mostly great growing up with such amazing people that would eventually feel more like family than family itself, we did have that one family 'friend' who would today fall firmly in the "Me Too Movement," a movement, calling attention to the assault and harassment experienced by women and girls. Many years later when I plucked up the courage to speak to a therapist about it, she acknowledged that this was sexual abuse and despite there never being any penetration I was molested in my formative years when I was still trying to figure out my own sexuality. I was horrified at the harsh words such as sexual abuse and molestation that the therapist used, but his behaviour was horrific, yielding cowardly power and control over a child.

"Hello, I'm sorry I don't even know if I'm calling the right person, but I saw your ad in the paper and it said if I'm afraid to speak to my family about my problem, I can call Helpline."

"Hi, you've definitely called the right person. What are you facing that seems to be stressing you, my dear?" The voice was kind and compassionate in my ear and the tears started to roll down my cheeks as if a switch had just been turned on.

"I want to know if there's any way that I can know for sure if I'm gay." She heard my voice trembling trying to get that short, emotional line out and she responded with relief, probably because she could have been speaking to someone wanting to end their own life, and even though this was the biggest issue in my life, it probably didn't rank up there with suicide which she definitely dealt with on a daily basis, I imagined.

"You could try dating some girls that you feel attracted to and see how that makes you feel, and you could try dating some boys and see how that makes you feel. You'll soon know which one you're most comfortable with. Does this sound like something you would be comfortable doing?" she asked with genuine empathy.

My 19-year-old Greek brain froze. "No, I could never go out on a date with a girl. I'm expected to marry a Greekman. Dating a girl is not an option for me," I replied helplessly, feeling worse than when I first picked up the phone to call Helpline. Worse and embarrassed because someone other than me knew my secret and what if they could trace my number back to me and somehow identify me as the gay caller. My mind seized. This was 1989 and I knew of no other gays. This was not a life I wanted for myself.

The rest of the conversation was a blur. She tried with all her training to get me through my turmoil, but at the end when we both said goodbye, I felt her dejection which was probably what she felt from me.

I was a confident young lady, but this stress broke me day by day. I would often wonder if anyone else could see it because it felt like the whole world knew I was a fake. I enjoyed the company of boys, once I stopped fearing them, and as I grew older, I actually got on better with them than with women, but it was always women I would be attracted to. There would often be the secret stares – gaydar as it's commonly known in the rainbow circles, but that made me panic and I would never cease the opportunity. I would hide and shy away and eventually decide being gay is not an option for me and I was going to marry a Greek man. I didn't want to disappoint my precious parents who sacrificed so much so that John and I would have the absolute best.

Men liked me. I just never knew what to do with that. I was tall, 1.75, which is tall for a Greek, pitch black, curly hair, blue eyes and the darkest olive skin especially in summer. The story goes that the original Greeks, going back to Alexander the Great that is, were all blonde and blue-eyed. My blue eyes came from my Yiayia though and the rest of me from Ba who was a striking man in his youth who did justice to the tall, dark and handsome slogan. My curvaceous Greek body, however, was an original copy from Ma who in her own right was regal in her appearance and her tall body, highlighted by her paler skin and auburn hair made men of all race and religion take a double take at her beauty and grace. John, who was much taller and more slender, was the spitting image of Ma and girls loved him, adored him and wanted him. He was definitely a favourite among women and a part of me envied his freedom to love with such ease.

Years later I would be a victim to hate because I dared to love my love.

Chapter 3
Mario

I'd been married for seven years. Not wonderful years, though to be fair, we had our moments of bliss. I loved him and I knew he loved me, but we were like oil and water.

You'd never say we had a difficult marriage having had five pregnancies and four beautiful children in six years.

It wasn't always like that.

I was a third-year student studying a Bachelor of Arts Degree at the University of Cape Town, commonly known as UCT, situated on the foot of Table Mountain's Devil's Peak in the city of Cape Town. Not something I was interested in to be fair, but I applied. I was accepted and so I did it. He was a second-year Engineering student. Not something he was interested in to be fair and literally applied the eenie meenie miney mo process of selection when choosing a course. He was a year older than me, but he elected to do his two year military training straight out of school so was effectively a year behind me at varsity.

It was a cute story.

"I can't believe I've just run into a school mate of mine." Patricia gleamed as she announced bumping into some American guy she went to school with. She drooled as she described him to Sue, Jane and I during our cafeteria lunch break, and eventually after a brief explanation of who he was, and how she adored him, we moved onto other topics before I headed off to swimming practice.

"Oh my God, girls, I have just met the most gorgeous American this side of Texas," proclaimed Delia as we were warming up for practice.

"That's so funny," I announced. "Patricia was just telling me about her schoolmate she bumped into today. How many Americans are there on campus? I've never met any in the three years I've been here and in one day, I've heard of two."

"Well, you'll meet him tonight if you come to the digs party, Irene. He said he might come. Didn't strike me as a party animal but I think I convinced him. Are you coming?"

"I am. Sue and Jane are picking me up, so I'll see you there." I was definitely not a party lover, but it was Friday night and everybody I knew was going, so I thought I'd tag along with Sue and Jane.

The party was in full swing when we arrived and we headed straight to Delia. She was proudly in full party mode and everything that came out of her mouth was a scream. "Here, Marco, here," she screamed at what appeared to be everyone at the party and then he was standing in front of me.

"Irene, this is Marco I was telling you about earlier," completely unaware she had his name wrong.

"Hi, I'm Mario." He held out his hand but it was whisked away as Delia pulled him in for a bear hug. I laughed when I saw his surprise. He was obviously not used to being mauled by gorgeous girls who were not holding back on social graces. I waved at him and turned to find Patricia had joined us.

"Irene, this is Mario I was telling you about today." He had somehow wrestled out of Delia's embrace and hugged Patricia hello.

"Hi," I said, still laughing at the chaos.

"So you've heard of me twice today?" he asked. "I did," I confessed. "How are you?"

"Nice to meet you. Are you Greek? My grandfather was Greek."

"I am Greek, yes, and I have been told you're American," still laughing at the clumsiness of it all.

The evening went off quite well. He hung around with us and he was definitely the flavour of the evening. Everybody wanted to speak to him. He seemed nice enough, I thought. He reminded me of my cousin George. He was much taller than me, dark hair, dark eyes and built well, but a build that looked easy for him to achieve. He was naturally muscular and was quite energetic. He looked like George so I guess he seemed familiar to me. That and the added factor of being Greek/American, a half European like me, and always retreating to me when he was given a break, encouraged me to go for a walk with him when he asked.

"Sorry, I just can't hear anybody in there. The music is so loud and I'm not a great dancer, so I prefer talking at these parties." I noticed but I didn't want to affirm his truths about his dancing skills to him.

We chatted and walked. We spoke about our upbringings and the coincidence of being at the same athletic meets for five years during our high school years. Me always rooting for his biggest competitor Jamie who attended my school, and him always beating Jamie. He confirmed that Jamie made him a better sprinter though. He was a star long jumper too and I recall thinking he should've made the Olympic squad with those distances. He later confessed that his first jump ever at primary school, he jumped over the pit and landed on hard grass. His coach picked him up and ran with him cradling him like an infant. "He's jumped over the pit. He's just jumped right over the pit!" Coach ran with him for about 15 minutes around the athletic track and that was the start of his athletics career. I thought he was naturally fit when I met him, and he confirmed it with his tales.

It was so easy being with him. He was an absolute gentleman and he made me feel safe and cared for. He spoke lovingly of his sister Katie and was so interested in my family. We lived in neighbouring suburbs, me in Sea Point and him in Green Point, so we arranged to visit each other.

"Are you going to the ball next Friday," I asked more out of curiosity.

"Do you want me to go?" he offered.

I giggled, not sure how that went South so quickly. "I mean I'm going."

"Do you have a date?" he asked sheepishly. "Do you have a suit?" I replied.

"No," he said looking rather disappointingly at his feet.

"My mom said I should pack it, but I just thought I wouldn't need a suit."

"We could get you a suit from a friend," I heard myself say.

"Thanks. I can buy one if you need me to."

"It's really just a once off event. I don't think you'll ever need a suit again. Let's see if Tony has one for you. He's your size."

"I don't think so," he joked nervously wondering if it was too soon to be making size jokes on day one. The truth is he always laughed at his own jokes. Took him a while to understand punch lines when others joked, but he would crack himself up at the telling of his own jokes. It was such an endearing quality.

We got a suit. It fitted. He looked smashing and he thought I looked exquisite. He made me feel so too. Hardly took his eyes off of me all evening. He went to get us drinks and came back with five drinks for me. "I forgot to ask you what you wanted and the queues were so long I wasn't going to miss my place in line, so I bought enough to hopefully cover all the bases."

A coke in case I didn't drink. A beer in case I did. A glass of wine in case I didn't like beer. An Appletiser in case I didn't drink but wanted to make it look like I did and a cider in case none of the above worked for whatever reason. I thanked him and we shared all those drinks and more throughout the evening. My favourite was and always will be Coke. I always joke and say I'm a Cokeaholic. I guess I have endearing qualities too. He confessed he wasn't sure how much money to bring to the event so he drew all his cash in his account. I laughed and knew he was creeping into my heart. We were easy with each other and I was at ease with him.

He always walked me to my door wherever my door was. He carried my bags. He paid for everything, always declining my offer to pay. He cared. He knew I was a virgin and I knew he wasn't. He wasn't putting any pressure on me. We spent our time getting to know each other and he seemed quite committed and patient with the situation.

He was kind and gentle the first time we made love. He was caring and sincere and we were in love. We loved each other through long distances and years of clocking time, eventually he decided we should be in the same town, two years later. We had spent a whole year apart because I backpacked across Europe when I was 21 after my graduation and when I eventually hung up my travelling shoes temporarily, I secured a job in the marketing department of The Marketing Firm in Johannesburg. He was in the process of completing his degree. So effectively, even though we were in the same country, we hadn't managed to secure the same province yet. He suggested we speak to our folks about helping us open up a business in building and construction. He was inspired by how busy his friends were that graduated years prior and money was important to him. He saw the profits they were securing and he started working on similar plans for the business. He was passionate about this idea and he convinced me to leave my then high paying corporate job which was a two hour flight from him to start our new business venture together. Our folks agreed to help and our lives began.

A year later we got married and in the same year we bought our first house for cash. The business was lucrative, our home was beautiful and we were ok for the most part. We fought quite a bit but I'd always put it down to the pressures of life and the drama that seems to follow continentals because of our passionate hearts. The following year our family started growing.

Chapter 4
Stefano (Stef)

Born in 1996, Stefano was our first. The ideal first. The one you secretly hope for as a first child. A son, to take the pressure of continuing the family name. A big, strong and bright boy, who broke all the expectations at every milestone. He grew fast, he spoke early. He used sentences before everyone else. He walked before he was meant to, largely because crawling was not an option for my big boy. He laughed a lot and still does. He was a breast-fed baby for over six months. Actually he was an-any-fed baby all the time. He, like me, has a love affair with food that will never be broken.

He grew with impressive abilities to grasp and embrace new challenges with ease and understanding. He would stand and inspect something until he was completely satisfied that he knew the workings of it, whether it was a toy, a freezer room door handle or a sibling growing in mommy's tummy.

He spoke a lot. He still does. He philosophises. I always say to him, his ideal career would be to sit on Mount Olympus pondering the meaning of life, while eating olives, bread and feta.

He taught me how to love in an expressive way. He taught me to hug and be affectionate. I wasn't always affectionate, but when your kid runs up to you and grabs you in a hug, I don't care who you are or what tough you think you're made of, you melt and you hug back and hope the moment doesn't pass soon. The hugs were always there. We'd sing and chat and dance and chat and cook and chat and fix and chat and play and chat and rest and chat. He loved chatting which was a great thing because he was the apple of his grandparents' eye. All four of them adored him. He was busy and he kept us on our toes. He was my first so we had all our first things together. First sick baby, first teething baby, first baby that breastfed. That earned him telling me what to do for the rest of his natural life from the age of "I can use my words."

"Mom, if one effort doesn't work, you have to try another effort." He would blurt out at the tender age of wise old four, every time I attempted anything and it didn't work according to him. As he grew, so did his vocabulary, but he always monitored and managed me. He was the oldest of many, mind you. It was his birth right and nobody would convince him otherwise.

He's kind and a genius, smart beyond words, wise and warm and funny. He's a legend. He's my legend.

Chapter 5
Boy or Girl

I was already pregnant with the second when Stef was only six months old. Yes, I was on birth control. No, I didn't know breastfeeding renders birth control as zero protection.

I had just discovered that I was pregnant with the second. I was excited. I was thrilled. Motherhood became me. I fitted into the role of motherhood as if all my lives and previous lives had trained me for this life as a mom. Doctor's orders were to stop breastfeeding Stefano because my body would not be able to cope with feeding him and growing a brand-new soul in me. That was done. Stefano went from breast milk to cow's milk in one swift move. Not sure he even noticed the change. I felt unwell. I went to the doctor and she explained that I'm losing the second soul. Went home and waited for it to happen and just like that, it did. Just like you eat a meal, or blow your nose, or brush your teeth, it slipped out and I was pregnant no more. I mourned a son I never knew. I always thought I was only going to be a mom to men. Mario was equally devastated and we were lost for words and actions for a while.

Days, weeks and months would pass and I'd feel fine and then out of the blue, a wave of tears and emotions flooded over me and it felt like the sorrow would never heal.I was unable to manage the onset and was always caught off-guard when it happened.

Mario dealt with it seemingly in the beginning when it first happened and appeared fine weeks later. He had an understanding of nature. He loved nature and he would just say, "It's nature's way of dealing with something that is maybe not strong enough to make it in this world." It wasn't comforting but he was trying to help me to heal.

"Try again," said everyone, "just wait three months for the body to recover." So we did, and we were pregnant again.

He or she was my first major loss. My deeply sad loss.

Chapter 6
Andrea

Born in 1998. Andrea was such a delight. He was tall and beautiful and calm and kind and still is. He loved his mom and still does. He's a gentle soul with so much love to give. His heart is gold and his soul is golden.

I feared the impact another child would have on my relationship with Stefano, but that was all in vain. From the moment he arrived, he was part of the team. In fact it was more like they were the team. Stefano would spend hours making him laugh and showing him the ropes. His adventure buddy. Their characters gelled and together they created their own calm in a world filled with chaos.

Stef would spend hours playing with Andrea and always trying to make him laugh and he would always succeed. Andrea adored his big brother and when he wasn't spending his time laughing at his big brother, he was quietly sitting in his baby chair and looking at his mom. Stef would pretend the baby chair was a mode of transportation and he'd play out the speeding, chasing game he imagined filled with sound effects and tipping the chair to almost heart attack mode for any adult supervising, but somehow, he always had full control and never dropped or hurt his brother.

They shared their father's passion for nature and they would spend all day outside with the pets, in the sand. They always had animal sets and that's all they ever wanted. Horses, pigs, cows, domestic animals, birds, wild animals, dinosaurs, any animal.

Andrea was intuitive and still is. He can understand every person's emotion, thinking or feeling by the words they use to express themselves. He sheds such clarity on arguments or difficult situations and he has empathy for all. He's the one who quietly watches and notices everything as it's playing out. He's very protective of his mom and siblingsand becomes enraged to a point of self-destruction if he sees his own tribe are hurt.

The most beautiful quality the two boys share is their sense of humour. I swear they laugh themselves out of every difficult situation and it works. Testimony that laughter is the best medicine.

He's kind and street smart and funny and is definitely an animal whisperer. He's a champion, my champion.

Chapter 7
Sofia

Born in 1999. Sofia was our baby girl. What? I thought I was only going to mom men. She's not a man. She's gorgeous. She's fair and a girl, beautiful and a girl, gorgeous and yes, yes, a girl! Soft to the touch. Slow to move. Prefers a chat to a run. Prefers to be pampered rather than playing with sand and chicken manure. Prefers silence compared to making animal sounds. Oh, and what a display of sheer naturalness as her older brothers treat her with more tenderness and care and protection than they would each other. Who taught them that? Me? Nature? God? Whoever it is, wow.

When she was born, I re-mourned my second child for a while, because I had mourned a lost son. Sofia's birth made me realise I could've had a daughter, so I mourned a daughter. And for a while I was sad, until I realised the presence of my second in every way, in every day and all was well.

"She's more Greek than American," the American announced at her birth. A Greek Goddess she is. She has classical looks that embody beauty, grace and charm.

It's hilarious to see the effort her brothers put into making her happy all the time, and the very second they put the slightest foot wrong, only according to her that is, she turns on the screeching dramatics and the absolute shock on the boys' faces is priceless every single time. As wise men do, they turn and get the hell out of her way because she's capable of anything. She just as quickly puts on the charm again and she has them eating out of her hand within minutes of the war zone that played out a mere few minutes before. The interaction has always fascinated me because it's so natural.

She picked her own outfits out from the shop from the age of two and does so with confidence twenty years later. She's decisive, honest, creative and has a sense of humour that she's picked up from her brothers which naturally makes her warm and endearing.

She's kind and understanding and the best friend you'll ever have in your life. She quietly gets on with being super remarkable.

She's my saviour. My saving grace.

Chapter 8
Dimitri

All was well with the children. Mario and I struggled to be decent to each other. It was a relationship based on love and hate. When it was good, it was great and when it was bad, which was becoming more often, it was very bad.

We were pregnant again.

Born in 2002. Dimitri was born and I fell in love with his looks and his calm approach to life. To this day his siblings call him the most handsome of all. He was my miracle boy. Birth was complicated and after three natural births, I had to accept his entrance was going to be an emergency caesar. He came out beautifully without a care in the world and no clue of the fear and trauma we were all experiencing on his behalf only five minutes earlier.

I gave him a Greek name because I am Greek. I was done with my marriage and was in the process of ending it.

Dimitri had the most beautiful disposition. Nothing concerned him, he always remained calm and he constantly stayed positive. He was equally great with all his siblings or just playing by himself.

You'd think by the time the fourth came, I'd have all the answers. That's exactly what my fourth did. Prove me wrong.

None of the previous tried and tested processes worked on him. He was going to be potty trained on his time and no amount of coaxing, manipulating or bribing from his siblings or his mom would make the slightest dent on his schedule, his way, his time.

He was his sister's live doll, he was his brothers' horse or tree or prop of the moment. If he wasn't enacting something from his brothers' imagination, he was being dressed up and pushed around in Sofia's dolly pram. When they would eventually tire of him, which seemed like an eternity because he was so much fun to be around, he would quietly get on with enacting his own story from his beautiful imagination.

He laughed so much. He always had everyone trying to entertain him so it was easy for him. He'd just sit there and let everyone perform for him. He was so cute and still is. Such an adorable person.

He's kind and funny and a true hero in every sense of the word. He's my hero. My brave hero.

Chapter 9
The End

Neither of us felt loved anymore and love is what makes the world go round...or so they say. We divorced. We gave it our best shot. We tried and re-tried and kept trying. We tried solving it ourselves, we went for counselling, friends and family advised, but in the end (well it should've been the end), I stood in front of a judge in the high court and said we could not reconcile our differences and he ordered us divorced. Just like that. Like you eat a meal, or blow your nose, or brush your teeth, we got divorced.

Chapter 10
Sarah

It was on my birthday when my affair with Sarah was publicised. I was in the process of getting divorced when I fell in love with my friend. Dimitri was a few months old and I had just breast-fed him and put him to sleep. The older kids were playing outside in the swimming pool with my father when Brad drove up our driveway. My mom, who had helped me get into a warm bath to relieve my body aches from the cut and the breastfeeding, ran to see who was at the door.

"Hello, Brad." Silence.

Silence. Silence. I couldn't hear him, only her. "I can't believe what you're telling me."

"Is it true?" she asked me in earnest but prayed for denial after she ended her conversation with Brad and watched him drive away to ensure he did not stay and cause a scene.

I confirmed her fears and she was gutted. She'd just been told that Sarah and I were having an affair.

Sarah and Brad were happily married, still are I think. Their three children were the same ages as mine and our kids went to play school together. I never noticed Sarah. I never noticed much. I was just coping with every day, trying to make it better than the previous as my marriage was falling apart. I hardly ever looked up from my children's faces to see the people around me. Nobody mattered. If I did notice anybody, there would be the friendly greetings, the normal niceties but no brain registration.

"Hi, Irene." I looked up. It looked like the warmest Summer day and even that looked dull compared to her smile. We chatted. We chatted. We chatted. School started and we were still chatting. We finally ended off with her inviting herself on Sunday to my house with a promise of some Greek dessert to serve with coffee.

"Bring Brad."

"He'll be away for work." He often was.

My desire to be loved again and her desire to have an emptiness and loneliness filled, led to an attraction that was unpreventable. Through all my dark days going through the most acrimonious divorce, I smiled. "I smiled in my heart, in my eyes, right to my liver" as Ketut told Elizabeth Gilbert to do in *Eat, Pray, Love*. I loved and felt loved and through all the chaos of horrible, I was smiling. I was happy. I was cherished.

It is my belief that when you feel loved, as a child or as an adult, you are content. You feel safe. You feel incredible. You do better, you achieve more, you fear less, you become who you are meant to be. That euphoria feels so good, you chase it because you always want it. In chasing the good gut feeling, you fulfil your destiny and in the wonderful words of Maria Callas, "Destiny is destiny and there is no way out." Imagine that for just one second. We become who we are destined to be. Wouldn't that be a wonderful thing?

So the truth was out. I was done. I was devastated. My heart had shattered into a million pieces and the broken pieces died off. They didn't regroup or refix or remould to make my heart whole again. I am a transparent person. I always believe in being open and honest, yet somehow my life is all about mystery and secrecy and everything I don't believe in. So I keep my sadness from all and slowly try to make sense of even more chaos.

I wanted to tell the world that I loved Sarah and that Sarah thought the world of me. She begged me to keep it quiet so we would not hurt our people. Our beautiful people who did not deserve the shame this would bring on them. I agreed and kept the secret.

Someone saw something one day and said so to Catherine. Sarah's mom, Catherine, was a well-respected woman in her circles. She earned their respect by working hard to keep the garden centre business lucrative, which her husband Philip and her started over forty years ago. Lucrative in a highly competitive market was a tall order but Catherine was determined. She was widowed way too young and left to fend for herself and her four young daughters after the horrific accident ended Philip's life instantly. The drunk driver never saw the red light. Catherine had to pick up all the pieces, working hard to ensure their family name was held high, partly out of a strong sense of pride, and partly in Philip's memory. All that was not going to go up in smoke because her youngest daughter Sarah had a moment of weakness. The visit from Brad was to say that they would ensure Sarah never sees me again and that my parents were to ensure that I do not attempt to see Sarah again. The relationship ended for us. No contact was ever made again. No goodbyes were ever said. Just like that. Like you eat a meal, or blow your nose, or brush your teeth, we were never to see each other again.

Sarah was beautiful. Perfectly formed lips, framed by a sculpted jawline that I loved caressing when kissing her. Long, thick, curly, blonde hair that lay comfortably around her face and fell softly on her shoulders. Her green eyes were always transfixed on me and I loved the way they lit up every time I noticed her staring at me. She was slightly taller than me and even though she thought she was too thin for her frame, I thought she was magnificent both to the eye and to the touch. I can't say what she looks like anymore because I haven't seen her in twenty years, but I can only imagine she is as beautiful as the day I first laid eyes on her. Her smile always reached her eyes and they locked me in. She was a breath of fresh air, my confidante, my dearest person who I adored. Sarah was naturally beautiful, but she was always well kept too. She took pride in her appearance and loved pampering herself or anyone else who wanted to be pampered by her. Her stunning hair was always brushed in a style that would bring out her warm green eyes. Maybe that's not true. Her eyes stood out even if her hair was tied casually in a knot. Her lips were the perfect shape and the perfect red and they kissed passionately, intensely and sincerely. I always touched the end of her lips, where the two joined as one, they had their own smiling dimple. How incredibly sexy I found her. She had such sex appeal and she loved being a woman in love with a woman.

Sarah had the ability to be the most gentle, caring person and always was with me. She wanted to protect me from the world of hurt and she did so for so long. She was the tenderness I needed after a battled marriage. She was the one that built me up again, made me believe in myself, gave me my confidence back and loved me, really, really loved me, and I her.

She was an amazing lover and together we learnt the art and joy of making love to a woman. She was free with me and expressed her lust and desire for me and the more she expressed, the sexier she was to me and the need to be with her intimately would be overwhelming and we'd make passionate love for hours. She was able to get me to talk about my feelings more so than anybody else could. She sensed my mood and my emotions and managed me gingerly so that I would open up to her crying and laughing or just expressing and she would always share such wisdom which I put down to her being five years older than me. The truth was that we had a remarkable connection, and for a short while in my life, I felt whole.

Chapter 11
Cyprus

My parents' way of dealing with me was to put me and my four young children on the first plane out of Africa, destination Cyprus. Make a life for yourself here was the instruction. That's exactly what I did. Despite feeling lost, lonely, scared and completely broken, I rented a home, I bought a car, I got a job and tried to smile in my heart, in my eyes and in my liver. I missed Sarah. My heart ached for her. I was shattered. People speak of heart ache but that is exactly that. Your heart aches. Physically it hurts in your heart. This was intense pain because it was sudden and not of my doing. I rejected it and couldn't conceive of a life without her, until eventually there was a life without her. One week became one month, became one year, became ten years, became twenty years.

My divorce, was less painful, not because I loved him less, but because I loved him less every time we argued. His words were brutal and I couldn't comprehend how this sometimes gentle soul, became so evil, without as much as a warning. What did I do to bring this out in him? When he got like that, I became enraged. I sometimes wouldn't recognise the animal I had become when my back was to thewall. I hated it, I hated him and I hated me when we got like that. He hated it too. I could see. The pain was constant and so was the hurt and because it was my decision to end our relationship, I didn't feel it like I felt Sarah's loss. I woke up one day and realised that the man I loved, my first love, my only love for so long, was no longer my love and what we felt for each other was not love anymore. The love had died before the marriage. That hurt, as much as it was ongoing, daily and continuous, was an easier hurt to bear than the hurt that is imposed upon you suddenly. My relationship with Sarah felt so right for us but was so wrong for everyone else. My relationship with Mario was so wrong for us, but so right for everyone else.

I was divorced. I was living in Cyprus. I was doing the proper Greek daughter thing. Raising my kids, visiting family, going to church, weekly spoils at McDonalds or souvlakia at Costas Grill, employee of the month, everything that makes the world smile. I was still trying to smile in my heart, in my eyes and in my liver. Mario wanted to see our kids. He flew from South Africa and was going to say his last goodbyes to them as he was offered a covert military job. The job would take him away from civilization as we knew it, for a decade. He struggled to move forward with his life and our business after the divorce, so he opted to hire a manager for the business and sign up for war. We had the business operating like a well oiled machine so that was not a concern but I struggled to comprehend that he would not be in his children's lives for a decade. He had not ever seen Dimitri as my mom was with me in the delivery room when he was born. She was the first person in my life to see him, hold him and tell him, "Hi, my boy, you're so gorgeous and Mom and I are so happy you're finally here." Having not seen the other kids for over a year, his heart softened with the days that went by during his stay. I confessed my relationship with Sarah and not only was he forgiving but he was understanding of my pain and expressed regret at our marriage failing. He had begged me to not divorce him when I walked out of 'our' home. Our religion does not encourage divorce. He had offered me all sorts of solutions but none of them included divorce. All I wanted was divorce, so why was I speaking to him about reconciliation again. Why was I doing this again? Had I not learnt the lessons that had played in my head over and over again? It was a hard, brutal marriage and a worse divorce. Why was I talking to him about trying again?

He held a hand out and said, "I know your pain. I felt it when you left with the kids and I know your suffering." He was the first person to let me mourn Sarah. He was the only person who let me speak of my love for her. He understood and he cared and he cried with me. We spoke about our marriage and we spoke about our kids. We spoke about our business and we spoke about our families. We spoke about the good and we spoke about the sad. We spoke and spoke and spoke. That's why I returned to South Africa with him and the kids to try and make it work again. It was a mistake. It should not have happened because less than a day back in our home, we reverted to our old actions, brutal and despicable. The kids were older now, so they understood what they saw, and they were scared and tormented by this hurtful 'love'.

I had made peace with the fact that this was going to be my life. I was never going to leave him again. I was not going to tell anybody how difficult our life and love was. I was going to enjoy the few good days and I was going to be the most loving mom to my men and my princess. My love for them was going to protect them from all the hurt, so I lied to myself. I would pray at night that Mario would find another to love, because he deserved to be happy and so did I, but as long as we were with each other, it was never going to work.

14 February – Valentine's Day and we thought it would be a nice idea to attend the local Valentines party. Maybe to encourage romance, maybe to fix everything in our relationship, or maybe just to kill some time on a Saturday evening. We weren't sure, but we were trying and trying means trying so here we are. Hand in hand because that's what you do when you're trying. You hold hands, you chat, pretend to care about the millionth opinion he's offered that day to make the world a 'functional' place, maybe dance but not really because he doesn't like dancing…and then I meet her, I meet Emma.

Chapter 12
Emma (Em)

I recognised the signs and feared them. My heart was not going to survive more of this. So I put controls in place. There would be a friendship only. If it got too difficult to hide my attraction, I'd distance myself until I felt stronger to cope with the friendship. Admire from afar was my modus operandi. She was easy just like a Sunday morning as Lionel would say. That's Richie for those who don't know Lionel in my life.

Emma's drop dead gorgeous, and when I would drag my eyes away from her exquisite shape, to meet hers, I'd see her soul. A deep soul with the calmest blue light shining through her eyes, and the message was clear and simple, "just love me." How easy it was to love her from the first second I laid eyes on her. She has an impeccable physique, with dark auburn hair that wants to curl but is waved to straight and the bluest blue eyes when she's open and vulnerable.

Years after Emma and Derek moved to our city from Johannesburg, Em and I started a little ritual. We'd meet for coffee once a month at one of the local coffee bars. Emma had been offered a partnership at a law firm in Johannesburg soon after they moved to Cape Town. She had not applied. She was head hunted and the offer was too good to turn down. She and

Derek had decided it would be best for her to take the job and they would alternate flying between Cape Town and Johannesburg as his contract in the firm was not going to last for many years and he would transfer back to Johannesburg too eventually. So she did this. Emma worked in Johannesburg during the week and travelled the two-hour flight every fortnight so she could be with Derek.

Derek and Em were very ambitious and held off on having children. They enjoyed their lifestyle and their freedom and were both not ready to start a family.

Coffee once a month with her was my treat to myself. I was running two businesses at this stage of my life, completely separated from Mario, and the kids and I were enjoying our new home. I could withstand everything as long as I could spend an hour a month taking her in, listening to her voice and watching her be. She was so much more than physically attractive to me. She was intelligent, ambitious, sincere, principled, kind and humble. The latter trait she earned from her parents Theresa and Eddie. They were good folk, salt of the earth. She could only but be grounded and filled with humility with them as role models. Her stories of her family captivated me and entertained me for hours on end. I loved the way she spoke of her older brother Liam and her younger brother Craig. I was captivated and captive all at once.

The friendship had a solid platform because of our keenness to be so honest and open with each other. Way before our monthly coffee dates, she was my sounding board, my buddy, my easy time.

Soon after we met at the Valentines dance, I offered her the whole truth about my relationship with Sarah. The words started coming out and despite having only just met her at a previous function, the words describing my past flowed and poured out like air being breathed. I needed her to know my version of events before the locals gave her their own twisted tale. She knew it all. She could judge me if she wanted to and I almost had expected her to, as everybody else had by then. I suppose I felt that if she judged me harshly early in the friendship, I could walk away without having invested too much of myself in this. I had the experience with Mario to fall back on. He was the only one who helped me through my pain after losing Sarah, but soon after getting me back, he became brutal and offered the most despicable words explaining what should be a persons' most intimate moments, and turning them into something sordid, cheap and dirty. I didn't expect this harsh rejection from Emma, but I did expect a rejection of sorts. She never rejected me. She cared...deeply.

Chapter 13
Fear

"I need to speak to you about something when we meet up for coffee later," she offered casually months after we met on Valentine's day.

"Sure Emma, is everything OK?"

"Yes, just something I want to clear up."

When Derek was transferred to the Cape Town branch, Emma was offered a post at Fairhurst Chace Attorneys, a new and upcoming law firm in Cape Town, also the law firm that represented Mario in our divorce. It was off her performance at Fairhurst Chace, in Cape Town that earned her the partnership at Ambleside, Bailey and Paxton in Johannesburg, later becoming Ambleside, Bailey, and Johnson when Em agreed to their terms. Ted Paxton retired and the partners were following Emma's cases quite closely, because they'd heard of this brilliant attorney making a name for herself in the legal field. The Fairhurst Chace office was small and clicky. She didn't adapt well to the office culture as she was a true corporate girl with a broader mindset. As expected and even anticipated, they were going to ensure she got their version of the Irene and Mario saga as well as the Irene and Sarah saga. They didn't stop there. Why would they?

"Taylor and Debbie from the office think you're attracted to me." She dropped the bomb as I sipped my tea.

"Why would they say that?" I blurted out, half choking, half burning forgetting I had ordered hot milk for my tea, hoping my poker face was not being shown up as a hoax with the internal, raging fire within me.

"I don't know but what I do know is that I don't believe them and I don't care what they think or say. You have never made me feel uncomfortable or uneasy. I value our friendship and never want to lose it. I just wanted you to know that they came to me with this."

I felt embarrassed. Embarrassed because I was transparent. I could feel my face soften and light up every time I looked at her. How pathetic was I that I couldn't even control my feelings publicly when she was with me.

She could see I was upset by the confrontation but I couldn't tell her I had decided to walk away. I could not put her marriage at risk of my love. I could not put my family through the same torment again. I was not prepared to lose my heart to a love that would never be because she loved her man and she often told me how happily married she was. Just like that. Like you eat a meal, or blow your nose, or brush your teeth, just like that, I lost my only friend because I feared the repeated verdict so I withdrew entirely.

Emma had faced great sadness in her life, I wasn't going to add to it. Em always thought she was adopted. Why wouldn't she? She had found some adoption papers in her father's safe when she was thirteen and convinced herself they must have been hers. She had hardly scanned through them when she heard her father calling her to assist with her brother's homework. She always felt like she looked so different to her mom, dad and brothers. People telling her she was the spitting image of her father's youngest sister meant very little to Emma, because she had never met her and she didn't agree with that opinion when she looked at both photos of her aunt. Emma was tall compared to her parents and brother Craig and it didn't matter when others argued that Liam was taller than her. Her hair was a unique colour and she had never seen anyone in her family with the same hair colour, not even her aunt. She was the only one with blue eyes compared to the family's brown eyes, despite her father telling her, she had the same colour eyes as his brother Michael. She was the only left handed despite her mom saying to her, she was left handed too, it was just that at school when her mom was young, the teachers encouraged her mom to use her right hand, by hitting her palms with a ruler when she used her left hand. So she progressively became right handed. The comparisons could have continued forever as she questioned her birthright secretly. She was shy and an introvert growing up. Her confidence was shaky because thinking you're adopted shakes and breaks your confidence.

Cape Town was never going to be a happy place for Emma Johnson. When Derek came home to announce the move, she felt as if the rug had been pulled out from under her. How could she play happy house in the same city she lost her father so briskly not even four years ago?

She instantly recalled the worst night of her life. "Hello," she thought she said in a sleepy state as she picked up the ringing phone. At least she thought it was ringing. Was she dreaming or was it real, she was unsure.

"Hi, Em – it's Wendy."

Really? Em thought. It didn't sound like her. The voice sounded thick and her words were inaudible.

"Hi, Wenz?" came the involuntary greeting.

"There's been an accident. Dad has died...I'm sorry, Em, I can't speak. Please come. I'm in Cape Town."

The phone signal went. "Hello! Hello! Wendy? Wenz?" "Derek, wake up, please dear God wake up, Derek." "What's wrong, babe?"

How could she regurgitate those words? She certainly didn't believe them. She was never going to believe them. What cruel game was Wendy playing at? What the hell was going on?

Derek repeated his question as he saw his bewildered wife have a panic attack.

"Babe, what's wrong?" he pleaded as he handed her some Rescues to help settle her.

"Wendy called." she placed three Rescues under her tongue.

"Wenz? Yes? What did she want?" "She said..."

"What, what did she say?"

"She said...No! Derek, she must be lying." she continued to gasp for air.

"Lying about what, babe? Please tell me. You're scaring me."

Emma rejected the news and was never going to say those words out loud. Her brain shut down. This was not going to ever be news for processing. Her body, her heart, her soul, rejected this. Then and always.

Derek left his wife on the bed and hurriedly called Wendy. He couldn't dial fast enough. His concern was that Em had a bad dream and that he would be waking the kids and Liam up while calling Wendy. The voice on the other end soon confirmed that it was a bad dream, a nightmare, their worst fear. Dad had died.

Michael, who was two years older than Eddie, was by far the one sibling whom Eddie could always count on. He was his big brother who took it upon himself to always be there for his little brother. Every time Eddie called, Michael obliged. That fateful night Eddie had called Michael and asked him if he could fetch him from work because the car wouldn't start again. It was an age-old argument. "Get rid of that thing. It's older than you. It's not going to last forever," teased Michael. The response was always the same from Eddie. "I can't, dad gave it to me because he knew I could fix anything, so I'll continue fixing it" he would announce proudly grinning at his ability to irritate everyone with his stubborn streak especially on this point of contention. Michael arrived at Eddie's work fifteen minutes later and he could see Eddie was tired from the day. "You drive," said Michael. "Drop me off at home and keep the car until you sort out that heap of junk." "Cheers!" responded Eddie, relieved he had a solution for a few days. As they crossed each other in front of the vehicle, Eddie handed Michael his bags to hold while he drove. Michael sat in the passenger seat and noticed what appeared to be a gun in Eddie's unzipped backpack. He opened it and removed it from the bag. "What's this Eddie? You don't like guns, you don't know how guns work. What are you doing with this?" "Leave me alone Boet. I just bought it from a mate. We've had two burglaries in a month and I don't have any way to protect my family. It's harmless, there's no bullets. I need to get some this weekend and you can show me how to use it." "I don't know how to use a gun" shouted Michael, forcing it back in the overfull bag and just then something in the bag hooked on the trigger as Michael pushed it down forcefully. The gun shot echoed in his ear for what felt like an eternity. He smelled blood and saw it on him and when he turned to look at Eddie, who was slumped over the steering wheel, the hooter a consistent whaling in the dark, cold, winter's night.

Em spent the next few days after receiving Wendy's call, in and out of consciousness. She recalls leaving Johannesburg with Derek to go to Cape Town to meet up with Wendy and Liam.

Eddie's body lay in the police morgue for a week until the autopsy was done by the district surgeon.

Dr Vittorio was a respected surgeon in the city. He graduated as a civil engineer and after working on several construction sites in South Africa, he realised his calling was to be a medical doctor. So several years after graduation, he found himself back at university starting from scratch in a completely different field. Although he was new in his field, his maturity was respected by the local community and he was trusted by all. He had a lovely disposition. A big man with a warm heart. He personalised the dead. He knew this man had people he loved and who loved him. He felt the heavy sadness of the mother, sister, wife or daughter that had just a few days ago embraced the man that he was analysing.

The docket was thick and detailed and gruesome, but the short verdict was he died instantly.

Em had been to see a medium 15 years after her father's death and he confirmed this to her. His death was in fact painless and quite a surprise to him as his soul lifted from the scene below. Eddie and Michael are always with you, he stated easily. Michael died a short three months after the shooting. He had a heart attack. Some say he died of a broken heart. Others say the stress of the legal process killed him. Others say he died the day Eddie died. Em knew they were always with her for a while now because Irene had told her about a dream.

Chapter 14
The Dream for Em

"Can we meet for coffee?" It had been months since we last saw each other and the shame of our last meeting had settled.

Em was excited to see me again. It was quite rare for me to set up the coffee dates so she grabbed the opportunity and almost said "yes" too soon. I was meeting her at her house and everything was ready for a great date. Coffee date.

"I'm sorry I haven't been in touch," apologetically because I really was sorry, but this was for the best.

"Life gets in the way," Em offered forgivingly.

"It's taken me two weeks to make this decision, because I wasn't sure what to do, but I think it's best I just tell you about the dream I had."

Em had just finished making the coffee and ushered me to the outside table. The weather was perfect and autumn was the most beautiful season in Cape Town. The Oak trees lined the long length of Farquharson Rd and if ever you were confused as to what season it was, the Oak trees of Farquharson would deliver the truth. The leaves were golden brown and Em loved seeing the seasonal change in Cape Town. There wasn't much Em liked about Cape Town, but Farquharson's Oaks…and Irene, she definitely liked.

I knew Em had lost her father and favourite uncle many years ago, but the details of the accident were never a discussion point. How could they be?

"I dreamt of Michael and Eddie."

Em froze. Her head bowed in an attempt to hide her shock.

"They have asked me to convey a message to you." I soldiered on despite seeing her scared reaction. Her head stayed down. Her tears rolled down her cheeks and dropped onto her arms which were placed on the table, clutching her hot coffee with her hands, hoping for some warmth because the sun no longer made an impact.

"They know you're sad and that you miss them all the time. Even when you're not thinking of them, your heart is heavy with the burden of their loss. The regret of not saying goodbye, the lack of your understanding in terms of how it all happened for both of them on that fateful day, they understand it all and they feel for you, but they want you to let them go. They're free and fine and incredibly happy. In fact, as they were delivering the message, they were clowning around with each other and laughing. They looked so happy, Em. It was such a feel-good dream. I wish you would have felt their presence, it was buoyant and filled with a light and warmth that could only come from a happy soul that's found eternal life and they're enjoying their journey through it all."

Em ran indoors and closed the door behind her in the hopes that I would not follow. I didn't. After sitting there for what felt like forever, I heard the door open and out came Em. It was evident that she had been crying but I kept quiet and did not want to offer any more information that may take her back inside to deal with the hurt she was so obviously facing.

"When was this dream?" She needed to know the timeline. Details, specific details were very necessary for Em, not only because she had the mind of an attorney, but details were important to put this crazy puzzle together. Many pieces did not fit and that made her question more, probe more, investigate more, decipher more, but in the end, the pieces did not all fit, they never did.

"It was about two weeks ago." I cringed at the prospect of getting the detail exactly as it was. I felt the burden of Em's need-to-know, but the dream was actually the complete opposite of that. The dream was about letting go, giving it up, release, relax and live. Live with light and love and let it be.

"What do you think I should do?" asked Em more out of something to say while processing the message inwardly.

"I think you should listen to them," I offered a warm smile and shrugged, as if to say "what are your options?"

"They're very happy and if your pain is holding them back from something, then surely you'd like to let them go so they can experience their journey in full."

"What do you mean?"

"See it's as if you were going on a pilgrimage. It's a trip that you've worked and saved for your whole life. It's arrived. Departure date-today. You've got your bags packed, the dogs are sorted, the bills are paid, but then as you're about to go out the front door, you're stopped by Derek. He doesn't want you to leave because he'll be too sad. He cannot bear the thought of not seeing you for a few months. Can you still go on your trip? If you do, will you be able to relax, absorb and appreciate its beauty? Or do you go back, and console him and explain the reasons you're needing to go on this trip. Comfort him and settle him. See his smile as he sees you on your way, and then you can peacefully move on to the next phase of your trip. That's exactly what your father and uncle have done. They will always check in on you once in a while, like with this dream, but they want you to know more than anything else, they are happy and they are free and that the journey may take long, but you will always feel them and see them in your life. I think it's nice that they're telling you they're fine. More than fine, happy."

Rumi quotes, "Goodbyes are only for those who love with their eyes; for those who love with heart and soul there is no separation." She nodded and smiled.

"I know it's easy for me to say let them go. It's not my loss, I don't feel the ache as you do, I'm just the messenger and I think it's worth your while to consider their message." I offered her another smile, in a futile attempt to keep the mood light. I did get another nod from her this time.

"I wonder why they came to you?" she asked. "Oh, dead people often do."

Her mouth gaped.

"Sorry, I should explain. I think it's because your pain is so intense, you're blocked from getting any messages from them. You have put a lid on this pain, and if you had to shift the lid just slightly, you'd rupture uncontrollably and it would not stop forever, so the lid remains perfectly tight and on and does not shift. I'm more open to the spirit world because I don't put a lid on it, despite being encouraged by many to shut it. Different meaning but you get my gist. I had a similar incident with Katie's boyfriend Jack. He died in a vehicle accident. It started out as a bar fight and when he got into his van to leave, it is believed that he was chased by the aggressors who then veered him off the road, causing his vehicle to roll and he ultimately succumbed to his wounds."

Em winced.

"He came to me days after in a dream and as I saw him is how I described him to Katie."

"The coroner had confirmed the same cuts, bruises and wounds that I had identified to her when he appeared to me in a dream. The message was simple. I love you and I'm sorry for having left you."

Chapter 15
New Home, New Life

I needed a big house when I left Mario again for the final time, because we were many, and I needed to buy a home with no money. That was the reality of my situation. I had just purchased a real estate office in Cape Town and having had absolutely no experience in selling property, I attended a few seminars to make up for my lack of knowledge. The one seminar I recall, because it changed my life forever, was "How do you buy a property with no money?" Sorry, did I just say that was exactly what I needed? Thank you, universe, God, Mother Nature, guardian angel and Archies. Archies is my term of endearment for Archangel Michael and Gabriel who, I believe, guide me, love me and protect me in this life.

The course was all about instalment sales. This is basically a purchase that with a small deposit an arrangement is made to pay installments for up to five years towards the seller's bond. At the five years' mark, the purchaser needs to finalise her own bond. Five years would be more than enough time for me to grow my property business and secure a bond for the guest house I wanted to purchase. I came back from the seminar on such a high, because just last week, the home I wanted, which I had always had a love affair with, was on the market. A beautiful Cape Dutch style house with double gables and she was gorgeous. More importantly the main house would fit my family. It was also being operated as a guest house, so I could secure a double income, buy a house and be completely independent. My life was coming together quite nicely. I was running two successful businesses and I was loving my freedom.

The home had a wrap-around veranda which was common in homes built in the 1920s. That and the huge kitchen was the heart of this gorgeous home. We'd spend hours outside with the dogs or in the kitchen creating gourmet meals because our love affair with food was first and foremost. Two rooms in the house boasted their original fireplace and we'd take turns sitting in the lounge or in the entertainment area with the fires on during those freezing winter nights only Cape Town could conjure. We settled into a comfortable life with the kids. We had a nice routine, we loved our home and we adored our pets.

Years went by. Sometimes seeing Em, sometimes not, always wanting to. This was how we carried on for years.

Chapter 16
The Crack in the Armour

The phone rang and it was her. "Have I done something to upset you?" she asked tenderly but irritatingly.

"What, no, sorry why? What are you referring to?"

"You're avoiding me. If I've done something to upset you, please tell me so that I can fix it," she pleaded. "I miss you and I don't know why you're distancing yourself from me," she continued.

You don't know why I'm distancing myself from you, are you completely blind? Do you need the hints to be bigger so that they actually become suggestions? I thought quietly to myself.

"I really am not distancing myself from you," I lied and continued to blame work, kids and life for being hectic.

"I understand," she sighed, more frustrated than at the start of the call. If she had hoped to feel better after making the call, she certainly didn't. I was feeble and pathetic and should have declared my love and lust and desire to be her closest friend a million times over, but how could I? I did not want to be the reason her marriage failed. Mine did. Sarah's nearly did. I could not go through this again.

I felt sad. I hated making her sad. She deserved only good in her life. I was not the best thing for her. Derek was and she confirmed it every time I'd ask them how they were. The answer was always well. They're very well. They always walked hand in hand. They seemed close. They seemed connected. I did not want to be the reason that ended.

Months went by and no calls were made by Em. I called a few times in an attempt to dissuade her thinking that I was distancing myself from her. She was always cold and seemed to say the right things at the right time, but there was little interest in her voice. She always kept it polite and proper but it lacked warmth and I missed it. I missed her friendship. I missed her voice. I missed her warmth. She was the most real person in my life. She was grounded and humble and solid and I blew it because I didn't have the courage to confess.

I'd call more often in the hopes that I would get my friend back. We always spoke about safe topics but she had distanced herself from me and I feared I had lost her forever. I would call and she would be busy, so I'd listen to her voice while I was holding for her. She'd be instructing her staff on how she wanted the case prepared, or she'd be attacking her team for making an error in judgement which could compromise her cases. I loved her work voice. She'd eventually come to the phone, not realising I had just spent the last few minutes listening to her words as if they breathed life in me. At least her work voice had passion, anger, instruction, anything but cold and distant.

"Oh, hi, I'm sorry you had to wait." That almost sounded warm, because she couldn't go from an instruction voice to cold in an instant.

"All good?"

"Yes, thanks, just preparing for a case again." "I'm sorry, I'll call tomorrow."

"No, it's fine, I'm in Cape Town tomorrow." "Should we meet for coffee?"

"No, I've got plans, sorry."

And so it went for months. She was over the bullshit and who could blame her. I was gutted. Who could blame me?

Months became years and I was single for a while. The thing with curious women, who are straight, is that they want to experience. I was open to that, because I had physical needs too. They'd call me up for coffee, sometimes a meal and the questions would come.

"How do you know you're gay?" would usually be the opening line. "I'm attracted to women," I'd say repeatedly.

"All women?"

"No. Do you love all men?" I'd try to reason with them. "Of course not," they would almost always answer. "The same applies to me."

"Do you like me?"

Here we go again, I thought. Yes, because that would always give them the confidence to continue and so they did. But once or twice a month, I'd call my soulmate. I loved calling her on her private line because I would always hear her work voice as some colleague picked up and made me wait while he informed her of a caller holding. She was often too busy to speak to me, but at least I could hear her in the background, and I always smiled because that's what you do when you hear your soul's significant other.

This time was different. She took my call and said she was good to speak. Shit, I didn't think that one through. What should I say? I just wanted to hear her voice. Speak, speak about what?

"What have you been up to?" she casually asked "Nothing much" I claimed.

"I hear you're dating again."

"What?" I blurted. "No, Jesus, what now?" I was gobsmacked. I certainly didn't consider what I was doing as dating.

"Derek told me last night that you're seeing a married woman." Silence.

Silence. Silence.

"Who does Derek think I'm seeing?"

"Holly," she confirmed. She was not much for playing around or building up. She wanted the truth from me and she was waiting for an answer.

"Oh." I sighed. "Is it true?"

"It's not that simple." I squirmed. "Yes, it is. Are you seeing her or not?"

"Let's have coffee when you come to town next." I prayed she would accept my offer. "We can't do this over the phone and you have a case to finalise."

"OK," she agreed. "I'm in town tomorrow. Same time, same place?"

I was ecstatic. I couldn't remember when we last had a coffee date and I missed them so much. Reality soon kicked in and I froze with panic. Shit, fuck, damn, she knows about Holly. Also tomorrow, did she say tomorrow?

As always, she looked stunning. I was usually the first one to get there because her time management did not exist, but this time, she was there waiting for me. I obviously did not rush to get there, nor did a child before getting a hiding, but I did love seeing her again.

"Hi, you look great," I said naturally. "Hi, thanks. So do you."

Oh God, she's pissed, I thought, her eyes confirmed it.

"What have you been up to?" I said, instantly realising the error of my ways.

"Well, I haven't been as busy as you," she offered. "Is it true? Have you been seeing Holly?"

Not once did I think she sounded jealous or angry at my actions. She was, but I didn't pick up on that at all. I immediately just offered the truth as we both ordered our usual drinks. Hers was always cappuccino and the large one, because the caffeine needed to kick in. Mine was just tea, always tea. My liver struggled with caffeine early in the morning.

Chapter 17
Holly

My mind went to Holly as I bought some time to choose my words carefully. I did not want to hurt Em or discredit Holly in any way. Holly, fiery Holly. She was beautiful, sexy and playful. Her face framed perfection. She was a pampered beauty. She, like Sarah, loved spending time on herself and it always paid off. Personally, I loved the unkempt look too but she was proud and she would not put foot out the door until her thick dark brown hair was perfectly placed, framing her warm endearing brown eyes that often reflected such a sadness to them, but the spirit was alive and well and she could put up a fight with the best of them. She had beliefs and she stood by them. They were fair beliefs, so she did not think it too much to take on even clients if they missed an appointment or canceled at the last minute at her hair salon. She started the business with her inheritance after she studied and trained in Franco's Salon. Holly was always going to make a success of it. She had a razor-sharp mind and she wanted to prove to the best of them that she was capable of holding her own. Her own, she definitely kept. She was the face of the business so it was equally important to her to appear as the finished product as it was to feel good about her looks. Em was growing impatient.

"Holly was curious about being with a woman. She's got a personal issue with intimacy. She is unable to climax with her husband, Greg. She's started hating being intimate because it's uncomfortable and quite frankly not worth it for her. She's been to a sex therapist for this but nothing seemed to work. She was wondering if it was the same with women. We've seen each other a few times only. We have been discreet and other than a kiss and a make out, there has been nothing. We haven't considered intimacy yet because we're still having fun getting to know each other."

I felt terrible for offering Holly's secret so easily to Em, but I trusted Em and knew it would always stay between us.

"How did Derek find out?" I asked, bewildered that anyone even knew of this.

"You sent flowers to the wrong person and they read the card."

"Flowers?" I was lost.

"You were supposed to send flowers to Holly, I assume, because you spoke personally about the two of you. The flowers never reached Holly. It went to Hilda and Hilda's telling everyone willing to listen about this. The card is addressed to Holly and signed by you. You know what it said."

"What?" I was lost.

"Irene, just check your flower orders." Em sounded irritated again.

I grabbed my phone and my hands were trembling. I did send her flowers last week, and I specifically recalled she made no mention of it nor did she respond. As I scrolled through the Netflorist orders, I found my order. Em was right. The flowers went to Hilda who had bought a property from me three months ago and I had their details saved on my Netflorist account. Her name was listed just above Holly's in my addresses and I must've clicked on the name above hers. Oh my God. Holly was calling me.

I looked up at Em, she stood up, threw R50 on the table and left. Left me with my thoughts, my patheticness, my sadness.

"Hi, Holly. Yes, I'll come over now."

I was met at the door by Greg, Holly's husband. He led me to the lounge where Holly was sitting. The house was quiet and Holly couldn't look at me.

"How stupid are you?" she asked rhetorically.

Holly was known for her harsh remarks but somehow that didn't pierce as it would normally have. My thoughts were with Em and how I managed to fuck it up again.

"Sorry," I whispered.

"Irene, I want to know from you what happened with you and Holly," said Greg in an attempt to be authoritative.

"Nothing, Greg."

"The card does not reference nothing, Irene, Holly says nothing too" he shouted.

"Nothing in terms of adult behaviour, Greg. I'm sorry, I really am, but all it was, was kissing and touching. You know Holly loves you and I think she just wanted to know if it would be different with a woman. We never got that far Greg. I'm sorry I've hurt you, but Holly loves you. Speak to your wife Greg. Sort it out." I stood up and found myself walking out their house, thinking only of Em.

71

Chapter 18
The Envelope

I stopped calling Em entirely because how do you fix stupid? You don't. She was better off without me, I pathetically tried to convince myself. Days turned into weeks, turned into months. I only saw her from a distance in a mall while hiding myself to not be seen by her. She walked hand in hand with Derek as always, but she appeared to be distracted. The hand holding was there, but the body language painted a different picture.

A group of ladies had booked an evening out at one of the city's fundraisers. A local DJ and his team of men had arrived to entertain the ladies. I had forgotten about the event until I was reminded by Samantha that morning. I had rushed to end the call with her because a second call was coming in and it was Em.

My "Hello" was hardly audible as my heart pounding was thunderous.

"Hi, Irene."

God, I swear she has the voice of an angel. Angels' voices should sound just like that I thought. "Hi," I said cautiously, never knowing which way the conversation was going to go.

"We have this thing tonight," she offered immediately.

"Yes, we do." Sigh of relief. I didn't realise she was coming to this event and hoped my answer didn't sound like a question.

"Shall I pick you up?" she offered.

"Yes, please" was my short answer. She lived five kilometres from my new home, so it made sense that we travelled together. If she lived on another planet, it would make sense to me that we travelled together.

"I'll be there at 7." "I'll be ready."

Of course I was ready by 6 and to my surprise, she was at my gate at 6. She was never early. Always late. I ran out and got into her car.

"Sorry, I know I'm early." She sighed and looked sad.

Looked like she was crying.

"I'm glad you are. Why have you been crying?" I asked concerned.

"Should we go for a drive before the event?" she asked, avoiding my eyes and my question.

"Yes, that sounds nice."

She drove for a while in silence and I offered very little conversation because it didn't appear to me that conversation was what she wanted. She eventually pulled the vehicle to the side of the road, switched the ignition off, and sobbed. It took a while before I held her hand. I kept holding it and she let me. I loved her and I wanted all that made her cry to leave her forever. Just not me.

"I have something to tell you –" she sniffed – "but you have to promise that you'll never say."

"I promise."

"Three months ago, soon after our coffee date where you confessed about Holly," I cringed but she went on to say, keeping her vision directly in front of her, "I received an envelope at work. It was on my desk when I got back from the courthouse and it was addressed to me with red writing sprawled across the envelope "Private and Confidential.". It was late in the afternoon and everyone had gone home. I couldn't get my head to stop reeling over the week's work pressures. I needed to switch off. I picked up the envelope from my desk and opened it. I've done this a million times, Irene. The only difference this time was that the envelope was filled with pictures not papers, which took me by surprise. I got comfortable in my chair as I turned the photos over so they could reveal themselves. At first I didn't recognise the individuals because they were in compromised positions but then it dawned on me, it was Derek and a woman I didn't recognise at first. As I went through each pic one by one, revealing his sheer delight at his lover, his smiling eyes looking down at her breasts as he fondled them, his penetration, his mouth sucking the flesh on her neck, my hands started trembling, I started sweating, feeling nauseous and within seconds, I was vomiting in my waste paper basket. With every recollection of a pic, I heaved and purged and for three days I vomited, got hospitalised for dehydration and lost all belief that there was good in him. My life with him was a lie. There was no credibility. There was no respect for me as he continuously made a fool out of me and the life we built together." She looked at me.

"It was Belinda, Irene."

I hoped the confusion was not written all over my face but it must have been, because she continued with her explanation.

"I called a private investigator and asked her to follow up and confirm my husband was having an affair. She asked me if the photos had a code on them and I confirmed they had. She recognised the code and referred me to the investigator who was hired to follow Mrs Belinda Adams. The husband Mr Roger Adams had hired her because he suspected she was having an affair. He thought I should see the photos first because my firm would represent him in his divorce and the investigator identified Derek as my husband to Mr Adams."

"Irene, you won't believe how that shocked me to my core.

"Derek?" I asked with no more words to add. She nodded.

"He denies it but he doesn't know I have the pics." "How do you know it's him?"

"The pictures are clear." "What are you saying?"

"My husband is having an affair and he's hiding it from me. He's denying it. In fact, he's outright outraged. He can't believe I would even think that of him."

I stared on waiting for her to finish.

"I believe he's been doing it for a while. I despise his sad attempt to cover this lie, but more importantly I despise that he is making me believe that I'm mad. I actually questioned my state of mind. Irene I feel like I'm going mad. It's the only thing that takes up space in my mind. It's my every thought. I haven't slept in weeks and when I do, I dream of them. I'm in turmoil.

Silence. Silence. Silence.

"What do you want to do?" I asked.

I kept quiet as she pondered a question I don't believe she had previously considered and one she had no answer for.

"I'm sorry," I said honestly. I was sorry for the hurt she was enduring.

"Is that all you have to say?" involuntarily taking Derek's affair out on me.

"I'm truly sorry you're hurting."

With that, she started the ignition and drove to the event. We sat in silence for most of the night but I hoped she knew I cared. The evening was a joyful event but the men were really lost on me. Em wasn't though. Her eyes were really the windows to her soul. I see it every single time. She attempted to make a fun evening out of it, but it was clear that she was in turmoil. Despite being sad and preoccupied, she did not want to go home when the event finished at around eleven and many drunk women decided it was best to end the evening with more drinks at Samantha's house. Em was keen, so we went. I sat next to her at the bar, in fact I sat next to her all night. I stayed with her and spoke to her and teased her, perhaps flirted innocently with her, but not once did we broach the topic of the affair again. Well, not by two o'clock that morning when she eventually dropped me off at home. I grabbed her hand in mine, squeezed it and kissed her cheek.

"Thank you," I said.

"For what?" she asked. "For trusting me."

A week later, my receptionist put a call through to my office. I picked up… "Hello?"

"What's wrong with you?" she scowled.

What have I done now? I thought to myself. "I'm fine thanks," offering the most inappropriate answer to nothing she asked.

"You were one of two people I told about the affair."

"Thanks," I continued with my line of complete dumbness.

"Irene, for the love of God." Silence – it's better that way.

"Did you know Tammy spoke to me for about four hours after I told her about it. Do you know what you said?"

Silence – stay safe.

"Nothing!!! Nada!!! Fuck all!!! Tammy questioned me, guided me, advised me, comforted me and you said nothing. What's wrong with you? Don't you care?" she scowled.

Well, I've secretly loved you for the past decade, from the moment when I first laid eyes on you and have thought of you every single day since then. Not as a friend. As a lover, as my soul mate, as my wife, as my fantasy, as my best friend. So actually, I'm quite delighted the idiot has been exposed, because now you can divorce his sorry, arrogant, undeserving arse, and be with me. I will love you always. is what I did not say to her.

Chapter 19
The Broken Promise

Her willingness to make her marriage work was genuine.
She poured heart and soul into fixing the broken. The
uncomfortable conversations had to happen and in as much as
discovering those photos were earth shattering and gut
wrenching, it did open a window of opportunity to discuss the
taboo topic. At first Derek did not acknowledge the affair and
outright denied it. Her legal mind would not be submerged
though and she pricked and prodded until eventually even he
broke under her questioning. She did not let up. Not even his
military training after school could protect him from this
torture and he eventually succumbed to her accusations which
were based entirely on undeniable proof.

"You did have an affair, why won't you just admit it to
me? We both know it's possible. Derek, I've been with you
only and as much as I don't know what other men do with
their wives, I do know most men are all highly driven
sexually. I have a higher sex drive than you in our marriage
Derek. You must be getting it elsewhere. You show the world
you love me when we're in the public eye, to the point that
your affection smothers me, and then the second we get back
home, you hardly look at me, you never touch me and I'm

disregarded until the next public viewing. You're in love with another. I need you to be honest with me and please believe me when I say, I love you. Please Derek, please just tell me the truth, because I feel as if I'm going insane and my mind will not stop until you release it by giving me the truth."

"I slept with her once," he confessed sobbing. "I felt nothing. It meant nothing. I'm not in love with her, I'm in love with you. I was just curious to see if I was in love with Belinda from school still. I called her once and we went out for drinks. One thing led to another but I can honestly say to you I am not in love with her."

"I'm sorry, but I don't want to lose you and I don't want our marriage to end. I'll do anything to save our marriage, and build on our trust again. I know it'll require a lot of work and pain and sacrifice but please, Em, please believe me that I am sorry for lying to you."

He sobbed and for the first time in her life, Em realised he was small. It had less to do with his size than it did with his ethics and morals.

"You're still lying, Derek." "I'm not, Em. I promise."

"If you were not in love with her, you would have stopped after the first time. The affair was continuous, daily, several times a day, and I have the photographs to prove it." She threw the envelope on the table. "You are living a double life and for so long you made me believe that I was the crazy one and that I was the unreasonable one and that I saw skeletons in closets that weren't there. I nearly lost my mind and you let me. You watched me suffer and you let it continue. Who are you? What have you become?"

"Em, I swear, I couldn't say anything to you. I didn't want to hurt you. You know I'm a good man. You know this is unacceptable for me. You know I want to be with you only and I promise you I will fix this." He paused." What do you mean photographs?" She ignored his question as he reached for the envelope.

"How, Derek? How do you fix being in love with another?"

"What photographs Emma?" He reached into the envelope and pulled them out. He was horrified. He looked at each one and when he went through all of them, he faced her, sobbing. "Em I'm so sorry you saw these." He struggled to get the words out. He got up and walked away defeated.

Em reached out to me a few weeks later, more because she needed space from Derek but also because we were easy with each other. She needed a chat and a glass of wine, it always worked. She confessed to trying to give her marriage another chance but that she had put a condition on the table, he grabbed it, embraced it and accepted it before her words were out her mouth completely. They needed to go see a therapist together. I sat quietly as she reasoned with me, more as an attempt to convince herself, I thought.

"What do you think?"

"I hope it works out for the both of you," I proclaimed quite honestly. "I want you to be happy and if this works, then great. You've had many years of happiness with him, it's worth fighting for."

I once thought she had similar feelings towards me. The kind where you want to be honest and frank, but you're not for the sake of not hurting the one you secretly love. It took me back to my not so glory days.

Chapter 20
Em's Disappointment

Years prior to Emma finding out about her husband's affair, when I was still living with my ex, we both let an opportunity slip through our hands. You rarely get second chances in life to express your love to your soul mate, but we did get one, and we let it go.

I was officially divorced from Mario. My insistence entirely. I was living on the Mediterranean isle of Cyprus, raising my four and working my life. He came, he saw, he conquered. Months later we headed back to our original life in South Africa again. Nothing changed. Same house, same business, same relationship. I don't know why I thought this was going to work the millionth time, but here we all were trying again. This time no marriage. I soon realised life with him was never going to be great and he would be equally miserable with me. I was intent on not going through the chaos again. No separation, no fights. I made peace with the fact that this was my life and I was going to accept it and live it, for a while anyway. We were miserable. I was, he was, the kids were and the only people happy were the ones we were trying to keep happy. Parents, society.

He obviously needed more and found it in another. Had my prayers been answered?

"What's going on? I've just come home because I forgot my work file and you're at work an hour earlier than usual.

"I'm expecting an early delivery," he lied.

That night he confessed. He loved her. The reality was that I was so over us, I said "OK, what do you want to do?"

"I don't want to lose you," he lied again.

"So then what do you want to do?" I stated matter of factly.

"I don't want to upset her either, give me some time," he pleaded.

This bullshit went on and off for far too long. Looking back I realised the time wasted on the undeserving was actually what complicated life.

Driving past Em that morning was divine. I saw in my rear view, she pulled off to the side of the road, so I did too. We walked towards each other and the vision was always stunning.

She's tall, slender, gentle and divine. "Hi." "Hi."

"How are you holding up?" she asked earnestly. At that point our circle was wrought with rumours of his affair and I could not have given less of a shit. I was pleased she knew though.

"I'm good."

"Has he moved out yet?"

"Yes," I confirmed, "but moved back two days later," I continued. She looked shocked.

"So are you and the kids moving out?"

"No. I've decided to stay with him, and work through it," I blurted out the words unemotionally.

She judged. Rightfully so. She fumed. Rightfully so. As the title holder of my soul, she was entitled to react any which way she chose.

There was a short explanation on my part, but I don't think the words penetrated. She was enraged.

"Why are you doing this again?"

"Why not? I have four kids to consider and the house and the business and the families and so I'll give him a million chances if he needs."

I heard her words. They were tender despite knowing full well that she wanted to shake sense into me.

"Be happy, Irene. Be happy."

Those were her words as she grabbed me in an embrace and held me so close I could feel her breathing on my skin. "I am happy for seeing you" I whispered in her ear. She looked at me and kept her gaze unwavered. I stood there staring back. A hundred messages were passed telepathically but no more words were uttered. We blew our chance of expressing our profound love for each other, but the time was not right. Everything was a mess.

How strange life turned out. I prayed for him to love another because I knew he would never let me go. Every night in my married life and in my life with him after our divorce, I prayed and begged God to put someone in his way, someone who would soften him and love him as everyone deserved to be loved. She was the flavour of the month until she wasn't anymore.

I had left him soon after I met Em in the street.

Chapter 21
Help

Therapy went well for a while. Derek and Em went to see a therapist whom they both appeared to be comfortable with. It was quite ironic because their therapist was Sarah's cousin Annie. How did I get myself into these situations, I often thought.

The reason therapy was going well was because Em was attending sessions and not Derek. Annie, the therapist who came strongly recommended as she utilised many methods but embraced spirituality with healing too, was eager to assist the young couple. Annie suggested the two meet separately in the beginning and then she would invite them to sessions together when she felt they were ready. Annie sincerely helped Em with posthumously forgiving her uncle, coming to terms with her mom's depression, coming to terms with the fact that she may have been adopted, and later being subjected to a husband who she felt was not attracted to her.

It was Derek's turn to attend sessions alone before getting the couple in together. Derek refused. He claimed he was fine, he had proven his love to her. He loved her and no therapist was going to help him because he didn't have a problem. This made Em furious. She felt humiliated, and betrayed. Slowly but surely Em became numb. Numb to all of us around her, numb to work, numb to home life, just numb. She was returning to Cape Town less frequently, and she stopped him from flying to Johannesburg every fortnight. She seemed to be getting into a deeper coma every time I saw her and I hardly saw her. She never smiled and if she did, it never reached her eyes. There was a haze over her eyes, and her soul no longer shone through.

Chapter 22
Celine

Celine Dion was performing in Durban. Samantha called all the girls and set it up. All ten girls were going to fly to Durban, watch Celine perform and spend the weekend at the beach. I could not contain myself. I was going to spend a weekend with Em and see Celine live. One by one the ladies canceled and three months later, it was only Em and I going. We had chatted over the phone a hundred times about the plans, the concert, the trip. It was the first time I had seen her smile reach her eyes, her voice had soul again and she was slipping out of her coma and into a reality that was thrilling. We were concerned the Durban concert would rain out as it was outdoors, so in our wisdom we booked the Johannesburg show at Monte Casino. I was going to fly to her in Johannesburg, she would fetch me from the airport but we decided to stay at a nearby hotel so we could drink and not worry about driving. She had booked a hotel room for us. One room, two beds. We were so excited we could hardly contain our excitement. The day arrived. She called, sounding worried and I braced hoping my worst nightmare was not going to be realised. "My car is playing up. I took it in for them to check it out and they want me to keep it in for a few days."

"No worries," I said way too quickly. "We can take a taxi," I proclaimed.

"You sure?" she asked be musingly.

"Absolutely," I retorted. "See you in two hours, I'm flying out."

Yes, the weekend was on. I had no idea she opted to rent a car for the weekend and I was surprised she met me at the airport. "I rented a car" she said. "Short notice, short list to select from." She walked me to our rental and I giggled as she opened the Smarts' door. "It's a Mercedes you know." she proudly stated.

She drove. We chatted. We laughed. We touched the whole way, not because we were holding each other, it was just that it was a tight fit. It was an amazing trip getting there. A quick shower and straight to the concert. Parking was going to be a nightmare, she said. It was packed to the hilt, but then I spotted a space between two vehicles at our entrance and I was convinced that if Em drove straight in, we would be parked and not hinder anyone else.

Despite it not being an actual parking bay and that all the other cars were parallel parked, we fitted and all was well.

We laughed at our silliness when we got to the venue because it was an outdoor concert in Johannesburg too. We thought Monte Casino was an indoor area. Emma hardly went out in Johannesburg because she was in the city mostly for work. When Derek came for the alternate weekends, he preferred to stay in rather than be stuck in traffic getting nowhere fast. She apologised for not knowing Monte Casino was outdoors and confessed again giggling at her silliness, "I never go out in this city". What a treat to see her so alive again. Celine started with a bang, *I drove all night,* and oh my

God that just set the mood for the best night ever. I swear I thought I saw her stare at me in a way she never had before. Yes, there it was again. Panic set in. I was terrified. I could not mess this up again.

She was on such an amazing vibe and I was starting to panic. She had not left Derek yet. She had confirmed on the trip from the airport that they were not together in any way anymore and were keeping up appearances for all and sundry. Essentially separated without the actual separation other than her days in Cape Town. She still had many clients in Cape Town and so she still flew in to meet with them when they set up meetings with her. I simply could not have a Sarah and I repeat. It nearly killed me losing Sarah. It would kill me, losing Em. So I put on my coward cap and pretended to be oblivious to the stares and the flirting. I refused a meal at dinner and definitely avoided the wine. An hour after the concert had ended, she was really tipsy, happy and ready to throw all caution to the wind. I was not. I did not want to lose my best friend. So when she showered, I pretended to nod off and spent the whole night foolishly in my bed and she in hers. Regrets, I have a few.

Chapter 23
The Call, "HI, Irene"

"Hello," I was hoping my voice sounded less surprised than my thoughts. Why would Derek be calling me?

"It's Derek," sounded an insecure voice on the other end.

"Hi, Derek. Yes, I know. How are you?" I was asking more sincerely than I anticipated because his voice concerned me a little. I was hoping Em was OK but I had to sound calm and unalarmed by his unexpected call.

"I'm good, I think, I'm not sure. I'm sorry to call so late," the voice sounded faint as if preoccupied.

I couldn't stand the anticipation anymore as I blurted, "Is Em OK?"

"Yes, yes, no sorry, she is well. I just don't know what's happening to our marriage Irene."

"What do you mean?" Pretending to not know I already knew what was happening to his marriage.

"Em has changed. I can't get her to connect with me on any level. She's become really hard and unkind and sometimes outright brutal."

I was waiting for him to say why. He didn't, so I asked, knowing full well her actions were in response to his affair with Belinda and the lies that followed continuously for a long while, until she challenged her sanity. His inability to carry through his promise to attend sessions with Annie was the straw that broke the camel's back. As much as I had not expected him to confess all those details to me, I had expected a slight indication towards a stressful time in their marriage, but no, he made zero attempt at going anywhere except Em has changed.

"What's caused this, Derek?" "I honestly don't know."

"You honestly don't know?" I hoped he didn't pick up on the direct sarcasm thrown at him in that question.

"None. Do you know what happened? Has she mentioned anything to you?"

"No," I lied. "I haven't seen her since Celine." That part was true.

He continued on a twenty-minute rant about what a horrible person she had become and broke her character completely.

I kept saying, "I don't know her to be like that." Every time he brought another example to strengthen his case, I'd repeat, "I don't know her like that." Eventually I settled with, "I'm sure something's happened to upset her. Maybe you should just try and ask her what it is. She's not irrational, or impulsive. She loves you and wouldn't be acting like this if she wasn't hurt. Chat to her Derek, I'm sure she'll open up to you. You've always been best friends. Speak to your wife."

"I've tried and tried and have reached my limit. I'm honestly done Irene." His voice was filled with irritation and I wondered if I had caused that. "Look, the reason I called you is because I don't see a way out of our mess. I was wondering if you have a nice room available for her when she comes to Cape Town. I don't want her living in my house anymore."

Shock.

"I'll pay," he continued seamlessly. "I just can't have us under one roof. We fight continuously and it's just no good."

Silence. Silence. Silence. "Irene."

"Yes, yes, sorry I'm here, I just can't believe what you're telling me."

"I know. Everybody thinks we're the perfect couple, and we are, but something happened to her and I can't pretend to be happy anymore."

"Why would you pretend to be happy? I thought you were happy?" He was caught off guard, it was not my intention, it just slipped out.

"Well, yes, but I mean for the last few months."

"I have a room for her Derek, a stunning one too and she'd be very comfortable. I wouldn't accept a cent, but are you sure it's come to this?"

His eager response almost made it sound like he was quite ecstatic to get her out of the way. What was he up to? He was such a creepy character and this call just confirmed it for me. Although to be fair, in a toss-up between Derek and Emma, Derek was never going to win in my eyes.

"Yes, well this is the only solution. Thanks for your help. I knew I could count on you. I'll tell her she's with you from tomorrow."

"Is she aware you're calling me to ask for this?" "No, of course not, but I'll tell her now."

"Oh dear God, Derek, I don't think she'll take that well." "She'll do as I say."

"Look, the offer is there if she wants to take it up but you really need to speak to her about this situation. I really don't ee this playing out as smoothly as you think it may."

I was right. Tempers flared. Chaos.

"Did you put him up to this?" came the shriek on the other end of the line. "Do you two think you can play me like a fiddle?" she continued with no pause. "Speak to me," she screamed.

"Em, I was as shocked by his call as you were. I swear I thought he was out of his mind even discussing this with me without even confronting you about this. Please believe me."

"Why? Why should I believe anyone anymore?" she continued shrieking.

I was worried. I could hear she was speeding and crying and I was terrified for her safety.

"Em, come to me. I'll make us a nice cup of tea. We can have a nice chat. I'll run you a bath so you can settle and you can spend the night here if you want. Please don't drive in this state."

She cut the call.

I tried calling and calling and calling, but to no avail.

Minutes turned into hours. Hours turned into my scariest scenarios playing out. The phone rang.

"Em? Please God be OK?" My voice was sincere and she heard that.

"I'm fine. I'm sorry. I can't believe what Derek did and I took it out on you. I took it out on you because I'm so angry at you too."

"Why?" I sounded feeble.

"You know why, but I guess you haven't done anything wrong. Look, I'm fine. I'm going to be away for a few days and I'll call you when I get back."

"Where are you?"

"I'd rather you didn't know because you may just come find me and I need to be alone right now, I really need to be alone right now."

"I'm worried sick about you." I was sounding tearful.

"I'm sorry. Please don't be upset. I'm OK and I won't do anything stupid, I really just have to sort my head out."

"Please call me every day."

"I will," she promised before ending the call.

Chapter 24
Relief

"Hi, Irene."

"Hi. It's so good to hear from you." "I'm at your gate."

I flew out of the house and ran to the gate forgetting the remote. "Are you OK?" I screamed through the gate bars so she could hear me from inside her car as the engine of her Land Rover muffled my voice.

She got out. She looked tired and defeated but even in that I saw a tender beauty, one where the lines of life were visible on her face, but she looked more beautiful with them. "Are you OK?"

"Tired."

"Come in."

"You need to open the gate."

I ran back to the house, grabbed the remote, fumbled, dropped the remote, picked it up again, my urgency was causing more of a delay than had I just calmly walked back and opened the gate. *For the love of God, what must one do in this house to open a freaking gate,* I thought losing my mind for the umpteenth time.

"Hi."

"Hi."

We hugged. We held. She cried and so did I.

We made tea. We chatted. I ran her a bath and she fell asleep in my bed, in my arms and I held her all night as she slept the deepest sleep. She was at peace for the first time in a long time. She felt safe. She felt comfortable. She felt loved.

"I've never slept in someone else's bed with that person," she announced when she eventually opened her soulful, dark blue eyes the next morning.

"Well, usually there's a lot more action that needs to take place." I cringed and pushed on, "It's OK." I laughed nervously. "The sex will come."

"I'll make coffee," and left before she had an opportunity to realise what I had just said.

"Stupid, stupid, stupid," I chanted all the way to the kitchen. "What are you trying to do," continued the self-discussion, "scare her off? Huh?"

I came back to the room balancing the two coffees and I placed them quietly next to her as I watched her sleep on. She was exhausted. I took the light sheet and laid it over her body, careful not to wake her. I closed the door behind me and let her sleep for the rest of the day.

She woke at about three in the afternoon and came out of the room looking for me, smiling when she saw me and said thanks for the coffee but it's cold. We giggled and spoke for hours on end after many hot cups of coffee, sitting by the fireplace, soaking up the warmth in the lounge, and for a while, she seemed happy.

Chapter 25
Em's New Home

The evening came all too quickly and I was somewhat disappointed when she asked me which room was hers. The guest house was perfectly established with the main house in the middle and the guest rooms off the side and back of the property. The previous owners used some of the bedrooms in the main house as a source of income because they were strategically placed with their own outside entrances with minimum disruption to the main house activity. My family was large and so we used all the bedrooms in the main house and only offered the entertainment area as a sharing area with guests which served as the breakfast area too.

I had shown Em Lemon Tree, which was by far the nicest room. When I first bought the guest house, I renamed all the bedrooms and named them after trees. Lemon and Olive Tree were my favourite rooms because they're my favourite trees. Lemon Tree was the biggest and most comfortable and even though all the bedrooms were exquisitely colour coordinated, something about Lemon Tree brought everything together so beautifully and effortlessly and it was aesthetically appealing even to the uninterested. Everybody always commented on this room. I was giving her my best.

"Are you sure? Derek says you don't want to be paid. This is your best room."

"Yes, I'm sure. You're only here for four days of the month and I'd like you to be close to the house in case you need anything. Let me know your schedule a week before if you need to stay longer and I'll work around that. I'll give you a key to the study so you can access the main house any time you may need something from the fridge or pantry. Please feel at home and feel safe because you're with me now and I've got you."

"This is too much," she managed through an emotional break in her voice.

"It's my home. You're my friend and I want you to feel comfortable. You'd do the same for me," I offered in an attempt to make her feel at ease. "Look, if you like, I can put you in the gym at the back of the house, I'll throw a bed in there, no curtains because that's too much if you prefer not too much." I smiled.

She laughed unexpectedly, maybe too much for the meek attempt at being funny but I was always grateful to hear her laugh. She didn't do it enough.

It was settled. She moved into Lemon Tree.

My home was hers and we were comfortable being in each other's space. When she was in Cape Town, she didn't have so much free time. She was usually writing a piece for publication, or a speech she needed to give, so I didn't see that much of her. She wrote descriptively with such ease and I loved hearing her speeches as she tried them out on me first. She had an amazing command of the English language, as one should have when you're the partner of one of the most prestigious law firms in Johannesburg. Her legal publications were considered some of the best written works, and young law students in South African Universities were encouraged to read up on her writings. She was often invited to speak at universities and recently had been invited to speak on Ted Talk. Public speaking came naturally to her and she held her audience captive for the entire talk, mostly enjoying the question/answer session at the end of her talks. She claimed this was where she understood how involved the audience was and she always felt so privileged to end the session because of time constraints and not interest limitations. She was a successful career woman and could never regret sacrificing family life. She achieved year on and year, won awards year on year, and I beamed with pride at each achievement of hers.

Chapter 26
Flirting

It was nearing the festive season. Companies were implementing systems for the three-week shutdown from just before Christmas to just after New Year. A national shopping mall was opening up on the South Coast of Durban and Em was invited as a VIP to all the functions associated with the major opening. Her firm had handled all the legal aspects of the business and she represented them at the opening. She was incredibly busy and I hardly saw her for the better part of three weeks. She was attending all the events and the company had booked her in at the Oyster Box Hotel, Durban's majestic 5 star hotel situated on Umhlangas' beachfront overlooking the Indian Ocean and the iconic lighthouse. She said she missed me when we called each other and I smiled every time she said it. She was looking forward to coming home for a full three weeks to put this crazy year behind her and bring in the new year with new energy, love and light and you she said once at the end of the conversation.

Em's divorce was in process. It was going to be an uncontested divorce. They agreed on the major distribution of assets. A list was drawn up for the smaller items and even though Em was not agreeable on all the points, she opted to accept it and move on swiftly with her life. She did not want to delay anything anymore and despite it being a fairly amicable divorce, if there's such a thing, she wanted to be divorced from him for certain. He would call her once in a while and attempt a reconciliation, a promise of this and that, but she was not interested.

I missed her. We were quiet at the guest house and the real estate office was closing soon too because the deeds office and all conveyancing attorneys were closed over the festive season. We were winding the last bit of admin down before the holidays when my phone signaled. I received a text message.

"Are you busy or may I call?" It was Em. She never called. When I got that message, I always called her immediately.

"Hi."

"Hi."

"Are you well?" I asked because I heard she was in a large crowd.

"Oh my God, you won't believe the chaos at the mall opening. I was treated as VIP so I was allowed to visit all the stores I wanted to an hour before they opened to the crowds and you won't believe the deals I've picked up. I'm so excited and I wanted to tell you about it."

Actually, she wanted to tell Theresa, her mom, about it, because Theresa grew up with very little and in her married life with only Eddie working while she raised two energetic kids, she had to make a buck stretch and she could make a buck stretch. Em was always so proud when she announced the savings she had secured from shopping sprees. She never needed to because she was extremely flush but would always want to and then want to tell her mom about it. Her mom had passed away a short thirteen months before. I guess she felt equally good announcing her savings to me as I always made such a fuss about it. Truth be told, I was proud of her no matter what. She could've picked up a pebble on the beach and I would've thought she'd summited Kilimanjaro.

"I'm just feeling so happy. I've missed you and I want you to know I didn't think I would be happy for a long time especially because I am still grieving the loss of my mom, but I'm also in the midst of my divorce. I can't explain this euphoria but I'm so grateful for it because I haven't felt so elated in years. I was numb for years. Thank you for being there for me," she said endearingly.

I caught myself smiling, mostly because I loved her command of the English language but her words hit home.

When she spoke, it sounded like poetry, but her words were penetrating me more so now than ever before. She thanked me for being there for her. Wow, I knew I didn't need thanks. I needed her just as much and I was having the time of my life having my best friend and secret crush stay with me.

"I'm heading home tonight. Is that OK?"

"I thought you weren't coming home till next week?"

"I know, but I want to see you," she confessed. "Is it alright?"

"Absolutely." I celebrated.

"I'll see you in three hours. Just going to the hotel to pack an overnight and rush to the airport for my two short hour flight to you"

"Perfect, can't wait," I smiled and my voice sounded happy as if it smiled too.

As she boarded, we sent each other messages so as to help the time pass. The first message I received from her was, "If Julia Roberts made a move on you, would you be open to that?"

Naturally I responded. Then I pushed the envelope. "If Julia Roberts made a move on you, would you be open to that?"

"You'd be surprised, or would you?"

I read and re-read the message a hundred times. Were we still discussing Julia or were we discussing her willingness to try a same-sex relationship? My mind was in turmoil, thinking, over analysing, assessing, deciphering, breaking codes, just going bonkers. This is not a mind that spends too much time on one specific thing, you must understand. This is a mind that skims over things and moves on simply to the next thing.

The phone rang. It was her. Damn I took too long to respond.

"Hi," I tried sounding casual. "I've shocked you," she stated.

"I'm unsure of what it is you're saying I think." I sounded like a complete idiot to myself.

"I think you know exactly what I'm saying. I'm on my way to you. Only you – and I send you a message saying I'm open to things."

How am I so unprepared for this moment! I'm usually on top of my game, what is this chaos I'm demonstrating.

"You've got some time to adjust to my message before I get home. I realise it's a curve ball, but I'm about to take off, so I'll call you when I land safely."

"A curve ball!" I giggled. "More like a boomerang." I heard her laugh and that settled me.

"I'll see you in a bit." Her voice was sultry and I was fucked. I knew it. I was done for. She would walk through that door and I would be too weak to even attempt a denial especially since I regretted not making advances on her at Celine's concert.

The time dragged. When she eventually drove in with her car which she kept parked at the airport sometimes, I was a wreck. She parked her car and got out. I swear I thought I saw an angel every time I laid eyes on her. Her tall slender silhouette moved towards me. The moonlight shaped her every curve, and her eyes looked directly at me and they were not sending mixed messages at all. I walked towards her and I was excited to see her. She smiled and said, "There's a bus that's broken down a few metres from here."

The bus driver stopped me and asked me if I knew where his passengers could spend the night. "They're on their way here." As I looked up, a bus was at my gate.

"What?" I looked at her confused.

"I know, Irene, I want that too, but business is business as you always say. Their insurance is going to cover their meals and accommodation. Let's run with it and we'll be together later."

It was honestly a whirlwind after that. I recall showing people to their rooms, tending to dinners, they wanted the bar open and really they were just throwing money at me all night. When I let the last guest out of the pub, I locked up and headed straight to my room. There she was. All warm and cosy in my bed, fast asleep. I looked at the time and it was two in the morning. I didn't realise the time and with that I had a nice warm bath and snuck into bed right next to her. I put my arm over her and she moved her body into mine. She was fast asleep and yet in her deepest sleep she knew she wanted to be closer to me.

I woke up to a buzz of activity. She was not in bed and I went looking for her in the kitchen. "Morning," said Lilly, my chef. "We're very busy today, Ma" as they affectionately called me."

"Oh, Lilly, yes, sorry, they all arrived last night and I had to sort them out with dinner and drinks."

"No worries Ma. We're on it. The breakfast room is set and all the food has been placed on the warmers. Go back to bed, you had a late night last night."

"Do you know where Em is?"

"Yes, she had to leave, but she asked me to get you to call her when you woke up."

"Leave? Oh OK. Thanks. I'll go call her. Thanks for running with breakfast. I'll probably serve tea and crème or coffee and lemon in my state today."

Lilly laughed. She was such an easy character. She was never phased even under the most stressful situations. She would always remain calm and always produce the best meals for the guests.

"Hello."

"Hi. Did you leave?"

"Hi, I'm so sorry, I had to. I have a ten o'clock appointment this morning and I can't miss it. It's with the Mall Manager and she wants to discuss the legal budget for the next financial year."

"Did you come home just for last night?" I sounded confused.

"I came to see you last night and I'm so glad I did. I'm sorry I brought the bus passengers to you, but it was late and they were tired and needed a place to stay."

"No, that's all good," I reiterated. "Thank you for bringing the business to my door. I really appreciate it. I'm sorry it went on for so long and I was unable to see much of you."

"I slept so well. I always do in your bed. I woke up with your arm around me and I was pressed against your body. I hope you weren't uncomfortable."

"I don't think I moved then. That's how I fell asleep." "So you purposefully put your arm around me." "Yes, I wanted to. I did."

"Good."

"When will I see you again?"

"I'll be home on Friday for three weeks. I can't wait." "I can't wait."

Chapter 27
Theresa

Em's mom was many things. She was born the third child to Tom and Lucy and since the death of Tom, Maxine, his twin sister, adopted Theresa in an attempt to replace Tom. Theresa was the carbon copy of Tom and because Lucy and Maxine lived in the same neighbourhood, Lucy agreed for Maxine to adopt Theresa. She was struggling with Tom's death and raising three children was not easy for her. The other two children remained with their mom. Theresa grew up knowing this and it had a shattering impact on her even though she was loved by Maxine, she felt she was ripped away from her siblings. It was only years later that Em realised the adoption papers she found in her fathers' safe were Theresa's adoption papers. Theresa never spoke to her children about it. There were some rumblings but not enough to piece the puzzle together. After Teresa's death, when Em was clearing out her things, she found some documents that referenced Theresa's adoption. Em reached out to family members for clarity. It was just how her mind worked. She needed to get to the bottom of every situation plaguing her. Theresa was an introvert by nature and enjoyed being home watching her soaps and reading the latest Stephen King novel or any dark fantasy, science fiction and psychological suspense genre. She liked Stephen King for two reasons; firstly he wrote brilliant stories and secondly she loved the name Stephen. She wanted to call her son Stephen but when her son was born, Eddie's father Craig had just passed away and so in honour of his father, Eddie called his son Craig. Theresa thought they'd have more kids so she was happy to name him Craig. "I'll name the next one" she winked at her husband. With Eddie's father dying, he and Michael needed to support his mom financially and it was a little difficult maintaining two households with one income, so there was no possibility of any more children and Theresa happily settled for the two. She was a strong character and quite demanding when she wanted to be, but on the topic of children, she agreed with her husband that two was enough. She could see the strain he was under, providing for his family, but he never complained and was always such a happy man. He kept work stress at work but she knew her husband and even though they never broached the subject of work stress, she would pamper him with his favourite meals and let him watch cricket on weekends while the kids did their chores, mow the lawn, wash the car, groom the dog and whatever else Theresa could conjure up to keep them grounded. Theresa was always dressed to the nines when she went out, which granted was not very often, but when she did, her shoes matched her bag, her hair was done up and the makeup and nails were literally like something out of a magazine. She took pride in her appearance and even though she never flaunted it, she loved the admiring glances. It felt good to be looked at once in a while.

She married her first true love Sam and they had a stunning little boy five months into their marriage. He was named after Sam's father, Liam. The story goes that Sam came home from work one evening and said he was taking a walk to the corner shop for cigarettes. She smiled lovingly at him because she truly missed him when he went to work. "Don't forget the milk for Liam, please, Sam." He threw her a thumbs up and that was the last she saw of him. He disappeared from her life for years without a trace. She had opened a missing persons' file with SAPS and even hired a private investigator. Both came up with no clues. Twenty years later she picked up a newspaper because she recognised the name in the story. Sam Rogers was arrested for murder. He was alive and that's when it dawned on her that all those years of her worrying for his safety, was a waste, guilt-ridden because her life and that of their sons' continued, despite his unknown whereabouts or state of life. She had the ultimate faith in her husband and never considered that he would desert his young family. He must have gone into hiding and changed his identity, Theresa surmised. She never confirmed it. She wanted nothing to do with him. She had moved on.

Ten years after Sam disappeared, Theresa met Eddie and it was Eddie who helped her rebuild her life. She started trusting a little again, but always felt a little guilty for moving on when she didn't have closure with what had happened to Sam. Liam was adopted by Eddie and Eddie embraced and loved the boy as his very own. He was already 16 when Em was born and out of the house when Craig was born. Liam is a good man. One of the nicest men I've ever met. I was introduced to him once when he was visiting Em and Derek over Christmas. I was intrigued by his tales. He's a Game

Ranger and works for Aquila Safari in Cape Town and ensures the territorial integrity of the reserve. His stories of close encounters, and sad recollections of poaching made him the most fascinating person I had ever had the privilege of meeting. He recalled meeting his wife after an outdoor shower turned to a compromised scenario. Wendy was lost in the camp after deciding to go for a walk to clear her mind. She was deep in thought thinking about her options regarding her up and coming mastectomy the following week. She was a cautious soul and would do her check ups regularly. They found the lump on the right breast and after considering all the facts, her oncologist recommended a mastectomy. She immediately agreed and wanted it out of her body completely and immediately. The operation was scheduled in a few days and instead of staying at home worrying about the procedure, she booked a little holiday at Aquila Safari. A treat for herself. Liam had just finished his outdoor shower which was his daily treat to himself but on this particular day, had forgotten to take his towel. He looked around and rationalised that it was only a few metres to his tent, so he chanced the short run in the nude. He was looking on the ground, sprinting frantically to get some cover, when he heard her say "Hello". He stopped in his tracks as naked as the day he was born, looked up to find the most stunning woman he had ever seen. "Hi," he replied, covering his privates with his hands. "I forgot my towel" "Yes I see that. I'm a little lost" she countered. "Yes I see that." he whispered. "Perhaps I can get it for you?" She offered reaching for it on the tent pole. "No it's fine" he said, stumbling forward, standing on a stone and jumping up and down holding his hurt foot in his hand while everything was bouncing and swinging around. As she looked away to grant him some dignity, she handed him his towel, only for a pair of jocks to fall out, landing with the front facing up, with the large letters "I play with pussy" written on it and as she picked them up, the back revealed "Cats"

That was the ice breaker. Liam thought he was going to die of embarrassment and she just started laughing, uncontrollably, consistently, till she wept, and he was at one stage no longer sure if she was laughing or crying, but for Wendy, it was the most cathartic experience and as he stood naked watching her, he literally felt like he was falling in love with her. She eventually stopped with short giggles in between, held out her hand, introduced herself as Wendy and announced she was having a mastectomy. They married within the month and two years later, they were the proud parents of twin girls, Rachel and Rebecca. Theresa's only grandchildren.

In 1999, Theresa lost her husband and brother in law who for years felt more like her brother. Michael and Eddie were inseparable in life and so it was no surprise that they were in death too. She had mourned the loss of her two men and what made the pain excruciating and unbearable was the fact that Michael had not been on speaking terms with her at the time of his death. Michael went through phases blaming her for Eddie's diabetic condition. He would insist she cook healthier meals and she would insist she did but Eddie stocked up on chocolate, cakes and sodas. This argument was old and would reach different degrees of seriousness. "You're trying to kill my brother" he would scream at her when he was absolutely frustrated at Eddie's disregard for his health. When Eddie died in the freak accident, Michael stopped speaking to everybody. He couldn't face anyone nonetheless Eddie's wife and kids.

He kept thinking of those ghastly words he would scream at Theresa, and in the end, he was the one that killed his brother. Theresa and the kids tried to reach out to Michael, but he refused.

Em was always there for her mom despite it sometimes not being easy as she dipped deeper into depression. She would spend hours talking to her mom over the phone, visiting her at her home and treating her to her favourite meals at her favourite restaurants. She was a creature of habit and hated change in her routine, food or anything else in her life. Em was convinced she always left her mom a little better when she first got there, but by the time she got there again or spoke to her on the phone again, Theresa was deeply depressed again. So the cycle continued.

It was September 2009. Em was still with Derek but I had already moved to my new home enjoying my new life. I had not seen Em for months. I walked into the local supermarket and immediately saw her. In walking towards her, I sensed something was terribly wrong with her and I panicked as I picked up my pace. I had not seen her in months and the first words I uttered were "What's wrong?"

"I buried my mom today." She fought hard to hold back the tears but the fight was futile.

I held her tight as the tears rolled down her cheeks and my heart broke for her. I moved away from her a little so I could listen carefully as she regurgitated Wednesday nights' tragedy.

Theresa had moved in with Craig two years prior because she needed company and Craig being a confirmed bachelor, needed the company too. They were good for each other. They had an easy relationship. He was grateful for the company while she lived with him, but he loved his mom's cooking even more. She made a mean beef curry, Craig's favourite dish, actually any curry would win him over, and Theresa got it just right, always.

He came home after a late night at work, having just finished from a repair at Busby Publishers. Craig was a Mechanical Engineer and the only person allowed to work on Busby equipment. Dave, the owner of Busby and Craig grew up together in the same hood. Craig owned his own company but his only client was Busby. They kept him so busy, he had no time nor need to source new clients. When Craig got home Theresa told him she had been struggling with chest pains. "Mom, why didn't you call me? Let me take you to Casualties" "I thought it would ease Craigie but it's gotten worse," she explained gasping for air. He picked her up and carried her to the car. She was of slight build, and once he secured her safely in the car seat, he rushed to get her to Milpark. "I'm so glad you came home early tonight Craigie." He reached for her hand and sped through the city to get to hospital. When he got to the entrance, he started hooting and a nurse came running out grabbing a wheelchair. Craig picked his mom up, but she was limp. "I think she's fallen asleep" he told the nurse between sobs. "I need a gurney!" screamed the nurse as he turned to the entrance. A doctor came running out, felt for the pulse, checked her pupils and her heart beat with the stethoscope. He stood up from the crouched position, put his hand on Craig's shoulder and nodded his head. Theresa was declared DOA. Em had a panic attack when Craig called her with the news, and all she saw were blurred visions of people standing over her as she lay on the ground trying to get oxygen to her lungs. The one clear face she saw, was

Theresa's smiling down at her. The next few days were a blur and she couldn't recall much other than the funeral she attended today.

"Why didn't you call me?" I pleaded. I was so hurt that I wasn't a consideration for her but then again, I understood.

"Sorry," she said again.

"No, please don't be sorry, I'm sorry. I'm sorry for your precious loss and I'm sorry I didn't know so that I could be there for you in any way you needed."

She hugged me again and Derek pulled her towards the car so they could get home. "Can I call you tomorrow?" I begged.

"Please do." She looked over her shoulder and forced a smile.

Chapter 28
Check Mate

As mentioned earlier, it was nearing Christmas in 2010. Em had surprised me with a visit for the night and instead of sharing our bed, we just shared a bed. The bus driver and his passengers, despite leaving a chunk of cash which was more than welcome, proved to be quite a demanding crowd and when I eventually finished with the final guest at two in the morning, Em was sound asleep in my bed. Of course by the time I opened my eyes, she was long gone.

The days passed quite slowly but peacefully. All was good.

I was a Franchisee and often flew to Head Office in Johannesburg for business. I received an email, sent to all principals regarding amazing prices on all branded items such as pens, note pads, t-shirts and moving tape. The prices were slashed by seventy-five percent but the catch was for one day only. They wanted to sell the stock before year end stock taking. Without thinking, I grabbed an overnight bag, filled it with some items, called my secretary and asked her to book me into a hotel for the night and to send me the details. I could've stayed with Em, but Craig had moved in with her after Theresa passed away and I needed some privacy for what I had planned for the evening.

I called Em on the way out and explained to her that I was on my way to Johannesburg. She was so excited and she didn't bother hiding it.

"I'd like to take you out for dinner," I asked rather shyly. "Great," she said eagerly. "I'll pick you up after work, I'm just finalising some cases today so I shouldn't run late.

Craig is home today so you can just pop in anytime. I'll tell him to expect you," she said, planning the day in her head.

"Actually, I thought you could join me at The Sandton Sun?" It came out as more of a question than I had hoped. I wanted it to sound more like a confident invitation.

Silence. Silence. Silence.

"Hello, are you there?" Literally the sweat was dripping from my brow. My nerves were shot. "Are we doing this?" she asked in a quiet voice.

I sensed her anxiety.

"Well, let's go to dinner and see how the evening plays out, there may be a bus load of people interjecting our plans again." I giggled and heard her giggling too.

"Perfect," she eventually proclaimed and sounded somewhat more at ease.

I got to Johannesburg, grabbed a taxi to Head Office, shopped at the head office store, chatted idly to the team and headed out. All I had to do was wait at the hotel for her. One hour became two, became three, became four. She kept calling to apologise for the delay but there was an issue with the arrival of some important documents from court and she needed to wait for them. She was always very discreet when she spoke about work. She never divulged any information containing names or relevant details and she never discussed any cases with me. I loved that about her. She had integrity and she was professional. I pretended that I was fine with waiting, but the truth was I was getting quite nervous with every minute that passed. Her last call came at ten to six.

"I'll be on my way in ten minutes. Papers arrived and I've prepared the case for next week. I'm headed to you."

"That's good. Be safe when you leave." "I'm quite scared –" she surprised me.

"Don't be. We won't do anything you're uncomfortable with. More importantly I'm here for one night, I just wanted to see you. I want us to have fun tonight and if that means we have dinner and you call it a day and head home after, so be it."

I timed how long it would probably take her to arrive and stood at the hotel window waiting for her to arrive. I underestimated or overestimated the time and got it completely wrong. My head was not functioning normally. I stood at the window for fifteen minutes before she arrived, just soaking in the view and trying to remain calm. The view from the hotel room was of Sandton City and I splurged a little, wanting the best for us, so I got my secretary to book a Superior Room. It came with a Nespresso machine, because she loved her coffee, a TV with DSTV, which I was hoping we weren't going to need, a stunning bath and walk-in shower, which I was hoping we were going to use and a host of assorted luxury items, to make our stay more comfortable. When I anticipated her arrival, I smelled myself, not sure why, I had showered three times while waiting for her. The knocking on the door startled me despite me expecting it and

"I'd like to show you something before we go to dinner. Is that OK?" I nodded and followed her.

We drove in silence. She tried putting some music on but no song really paired well with the mood, so she switched it off. I liked her driving style. I didn't like most people's driving styles but hers was good. I felt safe. She parked at the top of a small rise and in front of us was the magnificent soccer stadium, "Fun Fact! Did you know The FNB Stadium in Johannesburg is Africa's largest stadium with a capacity of just under 95 000. It's affectionately known as "The Calabash" due to its resemblance to the African pot. It hosted the 2010 World Cup Final between The Netherlands and Spain. Nelson Mandela made his final public appearance here at the closing ceremony of the world cup and I think that's all I remember" she giggled.

"It's magnificent," I hollered with excitement. "I didn't know you were a Soccer fan?" I stated more as a question. "I'm not, I know you are, so I learned."

She leaned over to me, I felt her fingers under my chin, she gently tilted my head to face hers and she kissed me tenderly on the lips for the first time in forever. I responded when I felt her tongue spreading my lips and I let her tease me for what seemed like the shortest time.

"Dinner?" She smiled.

I nodded. I had no words.

Dinner was a lot of fun. We shared the Nachos Grande and topped it with grilled spicy chicken, paired it with 2 rounds of Tequila shots and a round of Bloody Marys. It was only when I took my eyes off of her for the first time that evening that I realised we were the only ones left in the restaurant.

"Oh dear, I think they want to close and we're keeping them."

She slipped out of her smiling trance and pulled a face and said, "Well we'd better get going then."

I paid the bill while she waited patiently and then she said, "You OK for me to spend the night with you?"

"Yes," I thought I sounded pathetic.

"I'm really nervous but in an exciting way."

"That's good," I said, feeling equally anxious. "It feels good."

We drove in silence but soon after we left the restaurant, she took my hand and held it in hers the whole drive to the hotel, even when speaking and using her hands to express herself. She only let it go when we arrived at the hotel parking lot. We walked to the elevator together, went up to our room, unlocked the door, and when I turned to face her, she asked "When did you realise you were attracted to me?" she asked rather shyly. "You had me at hello."

"Tonight?"

"The night I met you for the very first time. It was at the valentine's dance. It wasn't an attraction. It was deeper. You stirred my soul and it was as if I heard my soul say, oh, there you are."

"You never saw me for months on end," she exclaimed in sheer shock. "I thought you hated me. You confused me."

"Self-preservation."

"You…" she wanted to continue but I put my lips on hers and her voice disappeared. I held her for too long but I didn't want the moment to end, nor did she because she held back and we let the moment last.

I took her hand and led her to the bed. As we stood in silence I unbuttoned her shirt with slow, precise intent. When I slipped the shirt off her shoulders, I held her because I felt her legs were trembling and I had to steady her against me as my fingers maneuvered through her pants button and zip. I prompted her to sit as I went on my knees and pulled her trousers off, her shoes, her socks and when I looked up she was smiling. I removed her final items of clothing which left her completely naked and vulnerable.

"You're exquisite," I whispered over and over in her ear. Her skin turned from smooth soft satin to a carpet of goose bumps which enticed me to carry on. I looked into her eyes, stroked her hair and said, "Let me love you." She placed her arms around my waist and ran her fingers down my spine which forced me to arch my body in ecstasy and she loved the power and the impact she had over me. Her focus turned to my breasts and she fondled them, caressed, and kissed them. I let her explore because I needed to explore her body too. Sheer perfection I thought. Every dream, every image, every thought I had of her naked had now come to life and it was just as perfect in reality but with the element of real which surpassed any dream or image or thought. I worked my way down from her lips with my tongue, to her perfect breasts, sucking, probing, teasing and then further down to her naval which then brought an involuntary groan to her mouth.

As I headed further down she grabbed me and pulled me up. "I don't want you to do that," she said quite frankly.

"It's OK," I said. "I do. You'll like it" I smiled as my confidence came back. I placed her arms above her head, pinning them down gently and kissing them from her fingertips down to her elbow and then her shoulder. She eventually succumbed and I whispered "spread your legs." She did, instantly, and I placed my thigh between her legs and rubbed up and down against her form so she could feel my desire.

"I don't get wet," she whispered, "so please be careful when you go in."

I stopped, looked at her and showed her my thigh. "You are wet," I said with a smile, "very wet." She propped herself up to look again and gasped. I winked and continued to move down until I reached her pink lips. I ran my fingers down the sides, spreading her lips with my hand and I placed my warm tongue on her middle. She groaned as I moved my tongue up and down with gentle force. She was releasing juices and I had hardly started foreplay. My fingers and tongue maintained a rhythmic dance as she lifted her pelvis with excitement every time she needed more, more of whatever I was doing. She thrust her pelvis harder and faster against my thigh and I knew she was ready for me. As she moved her hips up, I moved in and she grabbed my shoulders and looked for me. I was right there, looking at her, moving up and down with her with every penetration. Every time I moved my fingers slightly out, she'd tighten up to keep me in and that's how we continued until she groaned with sheer ecstasy and she kept her hips up so that I could stay in, penetrate deeper and stay still while she throbbed around my fingers. Her throbbing caused her to open up even more and even though I was still through her climax, my fingers slipped deeper into her.

"Please stay in," she begged. "Please don't go out." I did stay in, and I kissed her cheek, her chin and her lips. She held me tight as she kissed me back, releasing soft moans.

There was very little sleep that night. It was a night of extreme desire and passion which just led to intimacy all night. When she made love to me and I climaxed, I heard her words; "I'm not as good as you but I promise I'll practise and I'll get better." She giggled with excitement.

"Oh baby," I said, "you're very good and if you get any better, my heart won't cope." She rolled over laughing. It was so nice to see that she was relaxed. She was happy. What a perfect evening I thought. We made love, rolled over and napped for a few minutes out of sheer exhaustion, rolled back and held each other and spoke about everything, mostly my feelings for her and how I tried to maintain a friendship knowing I was in love with her. She understood everything. It made such perfect sense to her. With every scenario she brought up I explained it through my experience and she felt such love for me. We chatted, made love, just held each other, nodded off, made love and that's how the whole evening went.

By the time morning came we were exhausted. I called reception and extended my stay for another night. I was in no condition to fly home. She called her office and cancelled all her appointments. We spent the day in bed chatting over coffee or a meal. It was easy with her because she was my best friend.

Chapter 30
Long Distance

We had declared our love, lust, trust, want and need for each other, and we were completely open about our feelings. She loved this because she had only known me to be closed and quite confusing. Now that I could speak about how I felt, she understood so much about me and held the deepest regret and sadness for never considering that I simply loved her as an option when she was trying to figure my hot cold state all the time.

The one thing that hadn't changed was that I was still in Cape Town and she was still in Johannesburg. She would still travel every time she scheduled meetings with her Cape Town clients, but always ensured we had a day or two to ourselves before heading back to Johannesburg. The sex was incredible. It always is in the beginning of any relationship, but I truly felt connected to her. Being her first female lover, she soaked this new adventure up with such excitement and glee. She was right, she did learn and she did become great and my heart barely coped.

There was such a sense of vulnerability to her. She showed it all and all I wanted to do was protect her and love her. Just love her. I too had a fear of being hurt again, but I trusted her completely.

We had decided to keep our relationship discreet because we knew it was new and we were still figuring things out.

"Let's give ourselves a year," she requested. "If we're still together, we should tell our loved ones. Let's not rock the boat for something that may not work." I was in full agreement with that because I was honestly concerned about being her rebound love. I knew deep down she had exited her marriage years before the separation but I was her first after her husband and her divorce. She kept reassuring me I wasn't her rebound love, I was her only love.

We would cherish each other from time to time and saying goodbye to her was becoming more and more difficult. I was always quite excited when my franchise had a seminar in Johannesburg and it meant I would spend more time with her.

Seeing her was always like seeing her for the first time. We would be so excited to see each other it was becoming ridiculously apparent that we were more than friends. None of us confirmed suspicions though.

I loved her. "I've created you," I would always say teasingly. "I put those long, luscious locks there and placed those blue, bedroom eyes above that perfectly well-shaped nose and full, symmetrical lips. That strong neck that holds that incredibly intelligent mind. Shoulders of a swimmer, lengthy arms which end in feminine well-manicured hands. Your pièce de résistance, undoubtedly those voluptuous breasts madam." I smiled with pride. I confessed I thought she had caught me staring at them when we would meet for coffee at least on four separate occasions. She denied ever catching me but I swear her tops were coming in lower and her cleavage was more exposed. "Anyway, moving on past the breasts," I continued, "not easy but here goes. Oh yes, the waist, the desirable waist I so often place my hands around and guide your rhythm when we make love. Your lady parts which drive me to insanity and ecstasy all at once, all the time. Your shapely, long legs which wrap around me with ease and then finally the most beautifully shaped feet in the entire universe. You're welcome my darling, I've created perfection!" She laughed so loud and announced in no uncertain terms, "You're crazy my love." "Indeed I am Agapi mou, crazy in love with you." She's gorgeous and I'm blessed, but the best part of her always was her mind. Her intelligence, her wit, her humour, her kindness and her ability to see the best in every situation. Her inside matched her outside.

Chapter 31
Ma

It was strange that my mom called at work twice that morning. I heard it was her because the staff always called her Yiayia. She would always do her rounds and chat to everyone before she called me on the phone. She loved everyone and they truly loved her too. When she spent time in South Africa she would always come with me to work and offer assistance or advice which I often cherished because she had a remarkable sense of business. It was all she knew after arriving in South Africa straight out of high school in Cyprus to come meet my dad and decide if she would like him enough to marry him. He wrote to her from South Africa when my Bapou Ioannis (his father) walked past my mom's house in Yialousa and stopped in his tracks when he saw my mom. The story goes that my grandfather fell in love with my mom and his son married her. My Yiayia Stavroulla, my mom's mom, was against the idea because her fourth and youngest daughter had just completed her schooling. My dad wrote to her and sent a photo of himself with the second letter. She liked the look. She promised her mom that she would go but if she did not like him, she would stay with cousin Spiro for a month and fly back to Cyprus. Her mom agreed. So it was a proxenia – arranged marriage with an escape clause, we always laughed and this always made Em giggle. They got married three months after she arrived in South Africa and forty years later, they decided to return to their Cypriot roots to enjoy some early retirement after raising their daughter and son, and securing a good income for their pension from their businesses.

"Hi, Ma. Why are you calling again? Is everything OK?"

"I just got a call from an anonymous caller. He sounded Afrikaans but I have no idea who it was," she said in her no-nonsense voice.

"Yes?"

"He asked me if I knew that my daughter was in a lesbian relationship with Emma." Silence.

Silence. Silence.

Why can't I be the manager of my own life? I thought.

"Is it true?" she asked for the second time in my life.

She sounded calmer than when she first found out about Sarah and I. My dad had passed away since and maybe because she didn't have to worry about the impact of this on him, she was a lot more tolerable. Mothers can always see things from their kids' perspective, but it is tricky managing the father's response to it all.

"It is true, Ma. I'm sorry you always have to find out about my partners like this, I truly am. I'm sorry. I didn't want to put you through this again. I really am so sorry."

"Do you love her? Are you gay now?"

"Yes, I do love her. Yes, I've been gay for a long time."

"Oh."

"I don't expect you to understand," I regurgitated Em's words, because we often spoke about my parents' reaction with Sarah and how I would like it to be completely different if it were to happen again. She spoke me through my anger and made me understand my parent's point of view which was difficult but yes I could understand them.

"I don't expect you to understand," I repeated and continued, "I know this must be a shock for you again. I'm sorry for the hurt I caused and I hope I don't lose you. I'd hate it if I lost you, it would be impossible for me to live without you. I hope we can resolve this, but I can't change and I don't want to. I love her and she's a woman but that's exactly why I love her." She could hear my voice breaking with emotion.

Silence. Silence. Silence.

"I know your head must be spinning," I said, "so if you need some time to take it all in, take all the time you need. If you need me to come to Cyprus so that we can talk about this, I will. Tell me what you need, and I'll do it."

Silence. Silence. Silence.

"OK. I'll take some time to think about it," she said in her heavy Greek accent which I adored and made fun of in a loving way my whole life.

"OK."

I immediately called Em who was in Johannesburg and told her what had happened. She felt bad that someone had done this to my mom. "We can handle our end, but she's a retired lady, leading a peaceful and quiet life in her country, minding her own business." She stated irritated.

"What did your mom say to him?" Em asked.

"I'm not sure," I said. "I didn't ask because I assumed she said nothing because of the shock of it all."

I was surprised to receive my moms' call the next morning at six.

"OK, I've thought about it," she said. I don't want to lose you, that is never an option for me and it should never be an option for any mother. I don't understand it but maybe in time you will help me understand it. For now, I want you to guard your heart and protect yourself."

"You have been hurt in the past and I can't see you hurt again. It breaks my heart. The pain you feel, I feel twice as much as your mother, because someone is hurting my child. I know Em, I like Em. She's a serious girl and I like her ways. She is a respected career woman as are you and you both have to protect yourselves from the gossip in the workplace. I have always regarded her as the best of your friends and I hope she makes you happy."

Silence. Silence. Silence.

Just like that. Like you eat a meal, or blow your nose, or brush your teeth, I had my mother's support. Unbelievable, I thought. This could not have gone better, I thought.

"Thanks, Ma. Call me whenever you need to get some clarity on anything."

"I'm sorry you felt you had to keep it a secret from me," she said, sounding sincere.

"I'm keeping it from everyone just to protect everyone for now, especially the kids, Ma."

"I understand," she said.

"Ma, what did you say to the caller yesterday?" I said. "Yes, of course I know."

I giggled.

"I'm your mother. I knew before he called. You talk about her all the time. You sound happy and I'm happy for you."

Chapter 32
The Accident

So our love was declared and our long distance relationship was sealed. Well long distance for some of the month and no distance for some of the month. It was amazing being in love with my best friend. There's such a sexual connection when you can connect on a friendship level first. The distance was covered through her mostly flying to Cape Town and on very rare occasions, I would travel to Johannesburg.

It was Wednesday noon when Em called to say she was done for the week and she was on her way to me. She had found a ticket with Airlink flying out of O R Tambo at 2.55pm and she was going to arrive in Cape Town just after 5pm. I was always so thrilled to see her earlier than anticipated. It gave me such a rush.

"Weather's dodgy, so I'm going to leave early and take a slow drive to the airport," she said.

"What do you mean by dodgy?"

"It's been raining all day in Johannesburg. Overcast. Nothing severe. I will take it easy though."

I finished off some admin as the staff came into my office one at a time to meet about this and ask about that when Em called again.

"Hi, Agapi mou." I realised I sounded so cheerful every time I spoke to her.

"Hi, baby."

"What's wrong?" I immediately picked up on the tremor of her voice.

"I've just had an accident, but I'm fine." She rushed the latter words.

"Are you fine? Where are you? Who's going to help you?" I assumed she must have just been outside O R Tambo Airport when I glanced at the time on my laptop at 1.45pm.

"I really am fine," she promised. "I'm just before the N3 ramp and Craig is on his way to help me. The tow truck is here already and two cops stopped the traffic and are attending to me and the traffic jam."

"You're on the highway?"

"Yes, but luckily the car eventually stopped at the side of the fast lane."

"Eventually?"

"I lost control of the vehicle, baby. It spun across four lanes of traffic. I thought the vehicle could still be driven, but all the wheels have buckled with the spinning."

"How are you OK?" "I really am."

"OK, keep me posted, I'm coming to you. I'm leaving now. "

"Thanks, baby. Don't rush, I'll be fine until you get here. Craig has just arrived." "OK. See you soon."

I looked up and Thombi and Penny were staring at me. "We couldn't help but overhear. Is she OK?" asked Penny.

I literally regurgitated what Em had said and picked up my keys to head for the airport, when Penny said wait. "Take five minutes. Have some sugar water. Let Maggie book the next flight out for you while you're here." Maggie, who peeked her head in after hearing the conversation, nodded at Penny and got onto booking me on the next flight to Johannesburg. "You're in shock. Take a minute, settle and then you leave, OK?" said Penny discerningly.

It wasn't really a question. It was an instruction. I was shocked. My hands trembled when I took the glass from Thombi.

"She'll be OK," Thombi assured me. "God is great. Have faith."

I was amazed at how quickly I had settled. It could've been the sugar water, but I think it had more to do with the fact that Maggie had secured a seat on the next flight out which was at 5.25pm with FlySafair. That meant I would land by 7.30pm and be by Em's side by 8pm. My chat with my friends settled me as well. In as much as we were work colleagues, we were really always there for each other. There is so much to be said for lady friends who are going through the same life as you, facing similar daily challenges. I loved these ladies and they loved me.

I left and took particular time and effort in being cautious. I wanted to get there safely and ten minutes into my drive to the airport, the weather had turned to overcast on my side too. The rain was getting heavier the closer to the airport I was getting. Em called to say the tow truck removed the vehicle from the accident scene and it was being towed to South Towers. Craig was taking her to Netcare Milpark Hospital for a check-up. It was definitely the best trauma hospital in the city and I was relieved they were heading there. Shock often conceals any injuries and aches one can experience from an accident, but once the adrenaline wears off, the pain is severely evident.

I let my mind wander as I sat in my seat and buckled up for take off, more in an attempt to distract myself for the next 2 hours and from fearful thoughts of Em. She mentioned her arm hurt, her neck and head and an area in her gut sounding like it was near the liver. Don't go Greek, I kept telling myself, something Em often told me. She'll be fine. Think of something nice. I took my mind to the day I met Thombi.

I was at our business chatting to my ex about some final details regarding our split. I noticed a beautiful, tall woman who had such a warm face enter the premises. She was in mourning as she wore the traditional black garment familiar with the Zulu tradition. More and more Zulus were leaving their province Kwa-Zulu Natal (KZN) and making their way to Cape Town, seeking employment and a better lifestyle. My ex looked up at her and asked her if he could help her. She explained she was looking for work and was wondering if he had any vacancies. He nodded and apologised and she turned to walk away. I was struck by a sudden urge to chase after her and that was exactly what I did. I ran and ran as fast as I could. My God, I thought, how fast she walks, I swear she just walked out of the office now. I eventually caught up to her shouting "wait!" She turned back and saw me sprinting towards her. She stopped in her tracks, held out her arms to almost steady me if I needed it. I grabbed her arms but more in an attempt to get her attention.

"Is something wrong?" she looked concerned. She was slightly older than me, I noticed. "No, nothing is wrong. I heard you're looking for work."

"Yes," she said shyly.

"Well, I've just bought a real estate company and I start on Monday. I've never sold a house in my life. Would you like to try selling houses with me?"

She grinned. "Yes, please." I laughed and so did she.

"Let's do this," I said and told her where the office was and that she should be there at eight Monday morning. I shrugged as I looked at her, as if to say, if you're there at nine or ten it would be fine too.

"I'll be there." She confirmed this as we stood on the pavement holding onto each other as if our future was co-dependant on each other and it was and she was great. She got there before me, but she let me walk in before her and as we crossed the threshold we laughed and hugged and continued to absorb all we could to become the best estate agents that suburb had ever seen.

Penny was equally special. I knew her because she managed the local restaurant in our neighbourhood. She was such a cheerful hostess, dressed impeccably and always professional and competent. She was impressive in suggesting flavourful options, paired with the perfect drinks and ensuring our meals arrived in the quickest time, cooked to perfection. I bumped into her at the supermarket and asked her where she was working now that the restaurant was sold. I noticed she hadn't been there since the new owners took over.

"It's been tough," she confessed. "I sell my tupperware and I sometimes go and assist my sister with her admin. I'm literally earning the least I've ever earned in my life." I was shocked.

"Why don't you consider joining our team and come sell houses. I'll train you but I know you'll be a natural at this."

And so she was. She opted to focus on rentals because even though the money wasn't as good as sales, it came quicker. She eventually sold and rented. She was a workaholic and a perfectionist, the perfect combination for success. Thombi was the best sales agent and decided to focus only on sales which I supported entirely.

The parking at Netcare was always a nightmare but I asked the taxi driver to drop me off at the entrance so I could get to Em faster. I ran towards the main entrance, asking for directions to the x-ray department as I was sprinting and within two minutes I was with Em and Craig. She was lying on a hospital bed and Craig was pacing when I got there. We held each other until all the emotions subsided. I realised the seriousness of the accident when she repeated the tale but with more honesty this time.

"I didn't want to scare you," she said. "The police saw the accident happen and they couldn't believe I survived and that as the car was spinning across four lanes of traffic, no other vehicle hit me. I could see the cars coming towards me Irene. As I was spinning, I kept thinking that truck was going to hit me, that car was too close to avoid hitting me and eventually I just looked down because I thought someone was going to crash into me." I started to cry again as I relived the story with her and felt her intense fear.

We sat in silence for the rest of the time as we waited for the radiologist's report. Craig hated hospitals so he kept popping out for a cigarette. When he came back from his third cigarette, a nurse came over to us and explained that the liver had been bruised in the accident and there was some trauma to the right shoulder. She confirmed the head and neck pain was due to whiplash and that the doctor was happy to release her as long as she took it very easy for the next few days. She expressed that Em would feel some stiffness but after considering what could have happened, she said, "I think you're one lucky lady and you have some pretty amazing guardian angels."

"Michael and Eddie," confirmed Em with a nod.

We headed home and she kept apologising for the accident. I was not interested in the apology at all. I was so happy and grateful that I was with her and that she was alive and well, considering the accident.

"We can't keep travelling like this," I said when we reached her home and I made her comfortable in her bed. I sat next to her and held her hand which felt so cold. I started rubbing her hand gently to warm it a little and said, "The more we're travelling, the more chances we have of being in an accident."

She looked at me concerned that I was considering ending the relationship. "I think I should consider moving to Johannesburg with the kids."

Chapter 33
The Move

The plan to start moving was taking shape. I was going to sell the house, and the business, so I could be liquid in Johannesburg for a new home and business venture. Thombi was interested in purchasing the real estate business so that went off quite smoothly, while I marketed my home. I had decided to try something new in Johannesburg and I was interested to see what was for sale once I got there and got the kids settled.

There was one condition to my move as she was unable to move to Cape Town because of her work commitments. I wanted us to invest in a new home that would in future accommodate my mom too if she ever got to the point where she wanted to live with us. She agreed. We got it. A stunning modern, double storey property, with a quaint granny flat that boasted it's own en-suite, kitchen and lounge. All the icons were strategically placed to offer maximum protection. The garlic at the gate was new. Even our Greek neighbours Nicholas and Stella asked about that. To be honest, it was a tradition I was not familiar with. It was Yiayia's idea and when Yiayia had an idea, it was executed without question from all. Stef was going off to university to study psychology and weed, Andrea was starting his eleventh grade at his new high school, Sofia was starting her tenth grade and Dimitri was starting his eighth grade of school.

All went well as well as could be expected. I loved living with her and I loved my new city. The kids suddenly became brilliant at school. I think as the new kid, you have more to prove and prove they did. Andrea made the first hockey and soccer team and his average picked up by over twenty percent academically. Sofia went from being an average student to being one of the top five year on year and she could do art as a subject which was essential to her studies. Dimitri made great friends and fell in love with Drama.

Em was happy in her new home with her new family and her law firm was thriving.

"Are you happy?" She asked me when we were alone at home, sitting on our balcony, sipping Bloody Mary's on a Friday evening. This was becoming our favourite ritual. "Extremely" I said, raising my scarlet glass, "And you?' "I'm in heaven Baby, Thank you!" she raised her glass and winked at me.

Chapter 34
The Business

"I noticed a pub for sale about 2 kilometres from here" I said thinking out loud. "I've seen it too," she proclaimed. "I've been there a few times and I always thought it quite nice, needed a revamp, but nice. The owner approached me once and told me he was thinking of retiring soon. Maybe that's the reason for the sale." she offered. "I think I'll go speak to him tomorrow." "You want to run a pub?" she asked. "Not sure. Why not?" I shrugged. Dennis and Denise were the owners, it's why the pub was called D & D. I introduced myself and gave them a very short version of my story and they gave me a very long version of theirs over many drinks and by the end of the meeting, we shook hands and said "It's a deal!" The pub was tired looking and dated but I saw and felt its potential. We agreed on the price, the terms and the takeover date. Em drew up a contract, I signed it and she gave it to them to have their lawyer look at it. They called me a day later and said the contract was signed. I got to working on a marketing plan and it brought back such good memories of my early career. Takeover date was imminent and so I arranged to see some businesses regarding furniture for the pub. I had kept my Close Corporation registered, so I was able to make use of some great deals on alcohol prior to takeover. Our double garage became a storeroom and had I stayed home any longer, our home would have been the pub. Dennis gave me the pub keys 2 days prior to takeover. "You've been amazing in this transaction. It's been such a pleasure dealing with you" he started reaching for the keys in his pocket. "It's yours from today. Denise is home tearful but knowing she's going to be happy tomorrow when she can have the kids over at our home and not the pub for lunch. We've invested thirty years of our lives there. Not a day more" he proclaimed. "You have lots to organise, take these two days to help you." I was moved to tears by the old man and as I reached for the keys, he hugged me and sobbed, "Take care of my baby" with which he turned and left. The banner on the pub was huge and bright and I loved it. "Under New Management – Opening 1 April – First drink FREE!" The website was working perfectly after some glitches and there seemed to be general excitement in the community about "To Tavernaki" opening. I decided to go Greek with the name because when we were all in Cyprus on holiday, "Tavernaki" was our favourite eating place. I loved the name because it translated to The Little Tavern and even though it wasn't so small, it had a nice homely feel to it. I was going for a comfortable ambiance, with a carefree and informal vibe. The perfect place to come and unwind, listen to some good music, share a drink and a meal with a mate and hit the dance floor if the mood grabbed you. Em was so proud of me. She often was and she often said so. I was moving tables and chairs around trying to configure them a day before opening, when I felt her arms wrap me up. I turned to face her, "I'm sweaty" I stated the obvious, "Just the way I like you." she claimed honestly. I laughed because her lines still worked on me. She had me move from work mode to rip our clothes off mode in about ten seconds. I grabbed her hand and led her into my office, locked the door behind me and as I turned to face her, she pinned me against the door, kissing me passionately as she ran her hands through my curly hair. She knew that turned me on. I placed her arms to her side so I could remove her blouse. She excited me and I couldn't get our clothes off fast enough. As I was unbuttoning her trouser, I felt my jeans give way. I grabbed her breast in my hand to raise it to my mouth but before I got there, I felt her go in me. I moaned with pleasure as she slid in and out of me and I moved my hips in unison with her body. She was turned on and wanted more. She took my hand and placed it down her trousers and as I entered and found her spot, she pushed her pelvis towards me, so I could go deeper. Together we penetrated each other in unison and we were building up at the same pace as our breathing and moaning grew louder. I breathed in her ear "I love you" and she came in my hand as I climaxed in hers.

"I believe the business is now ready to open its doors" she smiled. She directed my face with her hands and I was looking in her eyes when she said emotionally, "I'm so incredibly proud of you. Thank you for doing all of this for us." I was still savouring the moment and started kissing her neck which instantly brought goose bumps to her arms. I felt her nipples harden against my breasts and I stroked them with my thumb as she let out a groan. "Hello, is anybody inside?" "Oh shit, the beer delivery is here", we giggled and got dressed as I shouted "Coming!"

"Actually" she said "About that"

"Oofa Agapi mou, my heart." I kissed her tenderly on her lips, they were always a little fuller and softer after she climaxed and I loved kissing her. "Hey" she grabbed me as I turned to go, "I love you too."

Opening night was a hit as I knew it would be. I had brought Lily to Johannesburg to manage the kitchen. Her kids were out of the house, getting on with their lives, and her husband was retired. She had restaurant experience but more than that, I loved her cool demeanour. We quickly made a name for ourselves as a place to unwind, enjoy a cold one and enjoy a great tasting pub meal. Simple, quick and tasty. Emma suggested we have a Greek themed evening one night and I thought it was a fantastic idea. We booked a Greek band, some professional dancers, thousands of pottery, breakable plates and the menu was mezze. There was an entrance fee and booking was essential. We were sold out an hour after the marketing went online. It was such a hit that it became a regular event once a month at the tavern. The best was we had regular repeat customers and my favourite who would come at least once a week for a Black Label and a glass of white Chardonnay, was Dennis and Denise. "Black Label is not a beer Irene" he would state with every visit. "It's a Lager!" "I love what you've done to the place" Denise would say every time she came. "We chose the best buyer for this place Dennis. Remember I told you, she's the one when she walked in the door?" "Yes you did Denise, yes you did." "Have you decided what you're going to do for Emma's birthday?" asked Denise.

Chapter 35
The Party

All the kids and Em loved sushi and so it was unanimously decided that we would serve sushi at her birthday party and have the party in our new home. Em had discovered online, as she often did, a novel idea that a local restaurant would bring their sushi chef and assistant to your home, with all their ingredients and serving plates. The only condition was that they would serve a minimum of twenty people and they needed to use our kitchen. Well, twenty was an easy number for us because just our family was almost half of that. The kitchen was ideally situated on the lower level which was open plan leading to the lounge and outside pool area where the party would be held. The bar counter served as the perfect dishing up area and Andrea and Dimitri were the self-appointed barmen.

Em had decided she wanted something different this year and she was seriously considering inviting as always her family our neighbours, but also her work colleagues. She went about inviting everyone and everyone had responded with a 'hell yes we're there'.

She went shopping to get an outfit for the occasion and when she came out of the bedroom showing off her new outfit and new hairdo, my heart melted. She looked like an angel. I had specifically chosen to buy her Engelsrufer jewellery for her birthday. I had bought her the pendant with the sound ball and the story goes that when you're wearing your Engelsrufer and you hear the sound in your pendant which sounded angelic, your angels were with you. She loved this. She loved any sign that confirmed her father and uncle were always with her. She missed them dearly but knowing they were with her always, helped ease the pain. She had chosen soft linen pants with a matching soft top and she looked exquisite. She had been to the hairdresser who always worked magic with her thick locks. She looked stunning and I couldn't take my eyes off her all evening. Every now and then she would come stand next to me, put her arm around me, and whisper "You make me feel so sexy" and then kiss my cheek, wink and move to the next friend for some serious catching up. I didn't know most of her work colleagues, so this was a good opportunity for me to meet them and welcome them to our home. The sushi was a hit. Everybody loved our new home. The DJ had everyone dancing and the alcohol flowed. Joy was had by all. Real fun. So why, what went wrong so suddenly?

Chapter 36
Dear Diary

After the party, Em became a lot moodier. I sometimes noticed her being sad, or withdrawn. When I confronted her with it, she just put it down to work stress, or dates that corresponded with the loss of her family. She shouted at me once when I asked again and when she saw I was so shocked I started to cry, she embraced me and apologised. "I don't know what to do," I said through tears, "Nothing it's not you, it's me. I'm sorry, I just need to relax a bit more. Work is stressing me and I'm taking it out on you."

Dear Diary

I think we're in trouble. It's been three months since we've touched each other sexually and the only communication seems to be what needs to be said. I've asked her to watch her tone a few times. I've noticed when she is uncomfortable with a situation, she retreats. When she retreats, she becomes defensive. When she's defensive, she's not nice. She can land a line. It feels as if my heart is going to break and when I look at her with sheer shock because it happens so unexpectedly, she seems to be doing it in her stride. As if she simply took a breath.

Dear Diary

I don't know myself to be this person and I don't recognise Em either. I told her how I hated everything about my life today. I told her I hated how we were in our relationship. I told her I hated that we were so dysfunctional. I told her I hated not being able to talk to her, touch her, love her. I told her I hated making the decision to move to Johannesburg because nothing worked. I have never felt so beaten in all my life. I'm on my knees and I don't feel like she'll hold out her hand to help me up.

Dear Diary

Sex was just that last night. Just sex. It's never been like that. We've always made passionate love. Always caressing and kissing and touching and feeling and holding and loving. Last night was just a fuck. It was nothing short of sexual frustration release and then roll over and sleep. It was cold and it was new and it was not welcome. It looked like it was here to stay and I wanted no part of it in our bed.

Dear Diary

I'm definitely more defensive and in as much as I pretend I don't hear the bitchy undertones of her voice, I am broiling inside and ready to release a storm that would have the round earth flattened. We're walking on eggshells and we're not facing any issues. We sidestep everything and everyone in an attempt to keep the peace. There are no raised voices but it doesn't feel peaceful at home.

Dear Diary

I feel the end is nearing. We spoke about counselling but even though I was all for it initially, I realise now, I don't have the energy to work at this anymore. She needs more and I have no more to give. I need more and I don't think she has more to give. I don't think we'll be fine.

Dear Diary

It's two weeks until Christmas and I moved to the spare room. We argued, she removed her ring I placed on her finger almost a year ago and I moved downstairs. We have nothing left to say to each other that is nice or loving and the hurtful hates that come out of our faces are intolerable. I can't be making her so sad and she can't be hurting me like this anymore.

Dear Diary

Merry Christmas. It's Christmas and because Christmas is Christmas, I asked her to join me for Christmas lunch. It was lovely, light, peaceful, loving and we thought we'd try again. I agreed to return to our bed on condition we don't fuck again. She agreed. She hated that experience too. I didn't want any part of that anymore, nor did she. It was foreign and I was not comfortable with it. Within five minutes of her being in my arms, I started loving her and she took it all in. It was lovely and loving but she felt different. It was amazing but unfamiliar. It was Christmas, so I let it go.

Dear Diary

I'm 50 today and we have plans! I woke up to the sound of her softly singing Happy Birthday in my ear. We had breakfast in bed and lunch at our favourite Greek Restaurant. The day was so special because she stayed by my side and she was kind.

Dear Diary

The world is under attack. There is a disease that has infested every country on our planet and it is killing us. They're calling it Covid-19, the Corona Virus. We are in lockdown. We are jailed in our homes and we may not leave except to purchase food, fuel and medicine.

Despite nobody being allowed to go to work, Em managed to secure a special permit and continued working. I sense she's under immense pressure. I try to ease her stress. I try to ease her strain. I try to ease her fears. I can't. She explodes and becomes a monster. She's screaming in my face and spitting and frothing and she's lost all control. I sense the end is near.

Dear Diary

She packed her bags today. She's left. I go upstairs and her ring is next to my bed, again. She's taken it off again. I pack the ring safely away and I wait for a week. She does not return. I look through photographs and I wait for another week. She does not return. I go through social media posts and we look so happy and in love. She does not return for a month.

Dear Diary

I packed her stuff in thirty-three boxes today. I hope she does not return anymore. If she does, I hope it's to collect her crap and leave. I'm finally done. I hate the shame I am feeling. The shame because I feel I have lost everything.

I was about to lose my business because of Covid but Denise called me to tell me Dennis had died due to Covid. She was going to move in with her sister and she had no use for the money I gave them for D & D. She gave 50% back and said "pay me when you can darling, you're going to need it to get through Covid." Despite her kind gesture, I feel so insecure, so unprotected and absolutely mortified.

Em's obviously reached her limit and she opted to leave. I could not blame her. We were treating each other so badly. Worse than anyone should be treated. We weren't kind to each other anymore. We could not tolerate each other anymore. We had crossed all lines.

Chapter 37
The Aftermath

I gave it my all. I put it all on the line. I moved my whole life to Johannesburg for love and I know there was no other sacrifice I could possibly make before losing myself entirely, which already nearly happened. I'm angry that she's ended it. I feel enraged. I felt like I was in a dream for thirty days and for thirty days I did not shed a tear. I felt blocked. I was blocked. I was confused. I kept waiting for the nightmare to be over.

Stef convinced me to start meditating as a way to release the negative thoughts. I started with a little twelve-minute Isha Kriya meditation every morning. This was taught to me by Sadhguru. I started listening to more of his YouTube Videos and the whole process started to make an impact on me. I paired this along with Bob Proctors' mind development theories and I just started feeling better about myself and my situation. The tears did eventually come and when they came, they came and they came.

The situation since Em left and returned two months later, was not a good one. When she returned, she found her life packed in thirty-three boxes. She moved into the spare room and came home every single day.

We spoke about her potentially leaving and finding a rental until I sold our home, but she claimed this was going to be an issue during lockdown. I wondered where she stayed for 2 months, but I didn't ask. For the last six months Em was angry. I didn't want to risk angering her, by asking where she stayed.

The saying goes that distressed lovers scream at each other even when they're standing next to each other, because even though they're physically close, their hearts are far apart, and if they shout loud enough, perhaps their hearts will find each other again.

Days passed by and the situation went from wanting to make up to wanting to end it altogether. It was exhausting, taxing and toxic. We knew we needed to resolve this unhealthy state, but neither of us really wanted to let go. I kept thinking, we were two intelligent women, who could certainly problem-solve and conflict-manage so why were we not able to fix this.

I got into the Land Rover one day, when I was too exhausted to think of the consequences of being caught driving during lockdown. I found myself making my way to her office. We needed to speak, but not at home. The building was locked, so I opened the door with her spare key. She kept a spare in every car because she often forgot her keys. I was surprised to find the building locked and empty, but I figured this was work in Covid. I walked past the empty Reception desks and offices and made my way to the end of the corridor where her office was since she made partner. I heard voices but couldn't make out what they were saying, it sounded good to hear her laughing again. The door was ajar, so I opened it. It took me a while to comprehend what I was looking at. My first reaction was to run, but I was stuck to the ground as if rooted by an invisible anchor. She didn't see me, she couldn't have, her back was to me as she lay on top of another woman on the sofa. I watched her make love to this stranger for over a minute in complete silence. It was love making, not fucking. She was enjoying it and so was her lover. "How long?" I heard the words slip out my mouth involuntarily. She turned her head to face me and all I could see was a stranger. "Irene" she got up grabbing her clothes from the floor, her face red and sweaty. The other woman who I could see from my peripheral went behind her desk and awkwardly put some items of clothing on. I turned to look at her, "She was at our party in our house." I turned my head to face Em "How long?" I repeated. This time my voice broke and tears came rolling down my face. "This was the first time" she lied. "You're doing to me what Derek did to you." I said quietly but with hurt evident in every syllable. She stopped, put on her clothes as the other woman left and when she was clothed, she looked at me, crying too now. "I'm sorry. It's been going on for six months." "The same time we've not been able to be civil with each other," I said. She nodded.

Chapter 38
Cars for Emma

I sat in the Land Rover for hours trying to find a way to unsee what I saw. The image of the two of them was imprinted on my mind. I shut my eyes, I saw them, I opened my eyes, I saw them, I heard them, I smelled her. I forced myself to think of something else, because I knew I was going to go insane. I opened my eyes and focused on what was in front of me. That's all I could cope with. The steering wheel, the interior, the sunroof and so as I looked at my immediate surroundings, I thought back to the cars for Em. It was Christmas 2013. I had arranged for Thombi to place a big blue ribbon around the Volkswagen Beetle that I had bought Em for Christmas. It was bright orange and it was built in 1970, the same year she was born. Penny drove it to my house at midnight and five minutes after midnight, I woke Em up and said I heard something outside. She was dazed from a deep sleep but intent on coming with me to check out the suspicious sound. I walked out the front door, her following close by and pretending to be hearing something around the side of the house.

Em? Are you coming? Em?

"Irene, why are you calling me, I'm right here. Don't make a noise. Let's just go inside. This is scary"

I led her around the corner and her eyes remained transfixed on her dream car, with a big blue ribbon on it. She screamed and ran back up the stairs of our double gabled home. She was visibly shocked and whenever she was shocked, her breathing became irregular and I needed to calm her.

"What's that?" Gasping for air.

"It's yours, my love. Merry Christmas."

"No, no, it's too much, I can't," she blew out with efforts of inhaling but her lungs were still dissatisfied.

"Shh, I tried to calm her. It's yours, my love. Stay calm." I whispered. "Breathe in, hold 1,2,3,4 and breathe out. Listen to my voice, look into my eyes and focus on my words. Breathe in, hold 1,2,3,4 and breathe out" We repeated it a few more times and with that her calm returned and sheer excitement kicked in.

"Let's take her for a spin." She shouted. I giggled, wondering if we should take the ribbon off. We decided to drive with the ribbon still on.

We drove for over two hours around Cape Town. The city seemed more beautiful at night if that was even possible. We loved this city. She was the perfect combination of mountain and sea. Em drove the city flat so she could familiarise herself with her new vehicle and she smiled for those two hours continuously. That became our fun car, our let's pack a bag and go where the road takes us car. We loved her and we named her "Meg."

The second car I bought for her was a Porsche 911. I bought myself one too. Harry was a good friend of mine despite his lifestyle getting the better of him, we always remained close. Harry made money fast and lots of it. He was a womaniser despite being married to Jules who loved him unconditionally. He used to say "she's only sticking around for the money," "You're an idiot Harry" I scolded him. "She adores you." Harry was a gambler too and lately paired drugs with his alcohol addiction. He saw the signs and called me up one day. "I'm about to lose everything. Why don't you take the the 2 porches from me in lieu of the money I owe you?" I loaned him some money a year back because I truly saw the potential in his business. I agreed, and so we owned 2 Porches. She chose the red one and I loved the the white one. That was the vehicle that saved her life in the accident. Despite the vehicle being a complete write off, she escaped fairly unharmed.

The third car I bought for her, was not meant for her. I purchased a Mercedes C Class for my sales manager. We were going to brand the vehicle and it was going to be the start of growing the company and creating brand awareness. Em test drove the Merc with me the day we bought it and when we got home, she said, "Can't we keep it? It would be such a waste for the manager. It's a Merc and I love it."

"It's yours!"

Now here I am. No Em and in her car with nowhere to go.

Chapter 39
The Realisation

It was late at night and there were some logistics that needed to be addressed. I knocked on her door. She hadn't moved out. She opened it.

"Can we chat?" I asked.

"Please." she begged. She tried often, but I couldn't. It was the images that seemed to have remained in my head with no space for anything else, no other thought, no grace. We had to resolve some issues urgently, so I was forced to open the lines of communication. I led her to my bedroom and pulled out a chair for her to sit. I sat on the bed because I had moved everything out into the garage. I had nothing else to do, and somehow having less in my bedroom, strangely made me feel better.

We started speaking about the telephone line, the WiFi, the mundane everyday fluff that needed to be dealt with and then I opened up. Not sure why, but I went with it. She saw my eyes when she opened her bedroom door and I was faced with her new look. Cropped dark auburn hair with a fringe that had been kept long enough to leave over her ear or tucked behind her ear. Made her eyes appear softer, kinder.

"Your hair," I said without being able to complete the compliment. I was scared and my voice broke. She thanked me, she always did.

"When did you cut it, because it was illegal for hairdressers to operate during lockdown." I regained some vocabulary.

"I didn't," she smiled. "I fell next to a cupboard that contained hair dye and scissors and this is the result." She smiled broader.

That's my love, not funny, but always trying, I thought as I smiled.

We spoke about the days that passed, the years gone by. The hurt she experienced, the hurt I experienced and so it went on till two am when eventually I led her back to her bedroom and tucked her in, not having mentioned the affair all evening. As I turned to leave, she grabbed my hand "I've never hated myself more for doing this to us. I want to fix it, if you'll let me."

I wasn't ready for this. As days passed, my anger set in and the more she wanted to speak and proceed cautiously forward, which I thought I was ready for, the more panicked I grew at a potential life with her again. I hated that she suffered so much too. It was visible. She had become sickly thin and developed tremors. The person I saw in front of me tormented me because such a heavy responsibility weighed on me when I saw her vulnerability. It drew me closer to her, much to my detriment. Despite sending out signals I was ready to move forward, I clearly wasn't.

I was told by a therapist, it was OK to be angry at her, because up until now, I had been calm through most of the chaos and almost responded in response to her actions and not how I truly felt. I kept a lid on it, until those wise words landed and I heard them. "It's OK to be angry at her," and I was.

The images never left me, but I never told her how they affected me. I recalled the day I drove to her office, never suspecting anything. When friends and the therapist asked, "Is there someone else?" I'd always respond with "absolutely not". I had the utmost faith in Em. I trusted her so much that even while I was standing in her office, watching her, I couldn't register it was her. It took a while for my brain to see her. I could see what she was doing, but because I trusted her so much, I couldn't believe my eyes. I felt like my senses were deceiving me. I think that's why I just stood there. I couldn't comprehend the reality. She didn't need me and she certainly didn't want me. She had another. She chose another. She wanted another.

I found myself driving to her office again, mostly to relive the route and process the trauma differently. I opened the office door and it was unlocked, my hands sweaty and clammy, I walked passed the receptionist who greeted me with a friendly "Hi Irene, it's so good to see you again" I slowed my pace as I approached the end of the corridor, her door was open. I knocked "Hi" she jumped up and walked towards me, wanting to hug me but I stepped back. She saw fear in my eyes and she welled up. "Do you want to go somewhere else?" Em offered gingerly. I couldn't. I turned around and ran out of her building. As I got outside, I vomited on the sidewalk. I realised she had run after me when she held my hair back as I puked and she wiped my mouth with her sleeve. She stroked my face and wiped away my tears as I straightened out, and as I looked into her eyes.

I saw her eyes well up. "What have I done?" she whispered. I turned to leave. She called and called and eventually sent a message, "Please let's speak face to face." I kept my distance because I knew she had power over me. I always became weaker when I saw her. You do when you see your significant other, always. I knew it was better to not see her at all, so I could start healing, but when she said she would move out, I said, "I don't think that's the solution."

Chapter 40
The Talk

She approached me one day as I was making coffee. "Can I have one?" she asked shyly. The kids were getting on with their lives and she knew we were alone for a few days. I nodded and grabbed a second cup from the cupboard. I felt her staring and I felt ashamed. I didn't think I looked good to her anymore, my confidence was at an all time low, I had shed my weight and I felt as if my curvaceous body had been lost forever. My thoughts were made up of only the scene which I kept reliving, my skin was pale and dry and appeared wrinkly. Had I grown so old so quickly I thought. "I love you Irene," she said and I let out a sarcastic sound. I took my coffee and walked away. "I'm going to leave today if you don't speak to me." I stopped, thought about it and then walked on. "You weren't innocent!" she screamed. I turned around and looked at her waiting for more. "I needed more of you." "So you found it elsewhere?" I asked. "Yes." "Are you putting your affair on me?" I raised my voice walking towards her. "No that's on me. I have to live with that, I did that and I will regret it for the rest of my life, but I needed more and you were unavailable." "How was I unavailable?" I grew louder and angrier. "What more would you have wanted me to do? I moved my life for you, I started afresh, it demanded more of me, it was a new business, a new city, a new home. What more did you want from me?" "You" she said bringing her tone down, because she saw me losing control. I threw the coffee cup at the kitchen window and smashed some plates that were in the sink. I walked towards her and grabbed her shoulders and screamed at the top of my lungs "You had all of me!!!" She got scared and tried to get out of my grip, but I pulled her back and pushed her against the wall, "You had me, you chose her! I continued screaming. "Let me go Irene" she pulled away forcefully. "Let me go" she said quietly. "Let me leave." she meant our home for good. I stepped back sobbing, she dropped to her knees out of breathe again. "Look at me, look me in the eyes and do as I say," I whispered. She turned to look at me and I always had to be calm when she had a panic attack. She felt as if every breathe was her last and the fear in her eyes tormented me, so I remained calm and held her hand "Breathe in, hold 1,2,3,4 and breath out. Breathe in, hold 1,2,3,4 and breathe out." We repeated it about 6 times, it took longer to settle her today. I dropped next to her and we were leaning against the wall, she held my hand and I held hers. "Just breathe, don't die, I'll let you go if you want to go." She got up, walked out and drove away.

An hour later she drove back up the driveway and walked in with some takeout. She found me in the exact same spot, sobbing at the thought of losing her. Sobbing at our recent past. Sobbing at almost losing 'To Tavernaki'. She sat next to me, opened the container and pulled out 2 Tacos.

I couldn't recall when last we had eaten and suddenly on top of the chaos, we were hungry. She opened a Coke for me. It was my favourite kind, ice cold 500ml glass bottle. Coke in glass always tasted better. She opened hers too, and downed most of it in one take. We sat there in silence eating and drinking and when we were done, she stood up. I thought she was going to leave. She held her hand out, lifted me to my feet, walked me to the shower, removed my clothes and hers, adjusted the water temperature and led me in. She lathered my body, turning me on with every stroke, kissed my neck and fondled my breasts, she placed her fingers in me gently and I sobbed. I cried because I missed her, I cried because I thought I'd lost her, I cried because she loved another, I cried and cried but the shower water felt good and her body near mine felt good and her in me felt good. No words, just love. I let her stay in me for long, because I hadn't felt pleasure in too long, I savoured her gentle movements in me and when I opened my eyes, she was looking at me, wanting me. She was turned on and she needed me to be in her. I turned her around and found her labia through her thighs. I spread her legs with my knee and I went in, gently and shallow. She groaned and pushed her waist into me, wanting more, wanting deeper. I held her breast with my left hand, squeezing her nipple gently, with every slight inward movement of my right hand. I stayed shallow in her, because it turned her on, and to get me to go deeper, she would move her vagina down so my fingers were forced deeper in her. She moved her right hand behind her back and searched for me and even though she was not facing me, she found my opening and put her fingers in me as we moved together. She made little circle movements with her thumb to stimulate me and I did the same to her. As I started moving out to turn her around, she begged me not to stop, so I continued with the same rhythm and movements. She lifted her right leg up against mine and as she did, she opened up even more, and I went in completely feeling her throbbing orgasm from inside. She let out a loud moan and coupled with her throbbing I climaxed too, pushing my body closer to hers, so her fingers could go deeper. She leaned against the wall panting and I rested my body against hers till I felt strong enough to turn her around. She looked at me and moved forward to kiss me as the shower water warmed us and washed away the tears. She held me as she kissed me tenderly, and caressed me. I knew kissing her always turned her on, so I grabbed her hair in my hand and pulled her head a little back, kissing her neck and sucking her. I was always too cautious to leave a mark on her neck but I gave no fucks anymore. I sucked and sucked and she moaned for more. I went in again and as my fingers went in, I went down on my knees and I placed my tongue on her clit. I stimulated the area as she pushed her vagina in my face for more. My tongue moved up and down to get her to peak and as I removed my fingers from teasing her, I put my tongue in and she grabbed my hair and moaned again as she climaxed for a second time. She lean against the wall as I came up and her legs were trembling. She started to cry and I let her. She cried and cried and held her head in her hands. I opened her hands and kissed her mouth, tasting her inside still on my tongue. "Irene, I wish you knew what you meant to me."

Chapter 41
Therapy

I agreed to one session. I liked Matilda from the get go. She was easy. Easy was necessary at this point of my life. I got there a few minutes before Em did and so this gave Matilda an opportunity to get my background information.

The oldest of two. My younger brother lives in Cyprus with my mom and is currently going through a divorce too. My father is deceased and we've lived without his presence for sixteen years.

"What do you think went wrong?" she asked.

"I honestly can't tell you how it got so bad so quickly. Had you woken me up that morning and told me today is the day Em leaves you, I would have said you're having a laugh, you've got your facts wrong, and yet it happened."

Just then Em arrived for the session.

At one point Matilda called it couple therapy and I wondered why because we weren't a couple. We were in separate rooms still. Matilda explained to Em what we had covered in the time she was not there and she then asked us both for a brief overview of how we began and what we felt was our undoing.

Our stories seemed to be aligned for the most part except for the ending. Matilda explained to Em that I was confused at how it all came so undone so quickly and Em acknowledged that she could comprehend how that would confuse me. I told Matilda and Em during our session that Em was trying to pick up from where we left off and I was at point zero with our relationship. In my mind, there was no picking anything up. There was nothing left to pick up. There is nothing without trust. I was at the point of "Hi my name is Irene and this is the new me, a changed me, a me I no longer recognise and I certainly do not recognise the person I'm meeting." The confusing part of therapy was that Matilda kept repeating that from the very first session Em kept reiterating that she wanted to make this work. I could not believe the words escaping her mouth. "I challenge that," I said. "I think she is saying that because she potentially fears a life without me, but I don't think this is what she wants. She wants another."

"Honestly," said Matilda, "she repeats it every time to me."

"I don't believe her," I uttered in total honesty. "I simply don't believe her," I repeated to Matilda and then acknowledged Em again. "I challenge that."

There are ways you act, speak and think when you want to achieve something. You have to be aligned. Your thoughts must align with your words, must align with your actions for anything to be done. "Zarathustra taught the importance of good thoughts, good words, and good deeds,"

Chapter 42
Reunited

We'd been to therapy twice and honestly the best advice I got from Matilda was to float. Everything in my life felt so big, so scary and I was frightened of everything. "Just float," said Matilda. "That's all you can do anyway, that's all you need to do." So I did, I floated.

In floating, life became simpler. Communication became easier and Emma's birthday was nearing. Birthdays are birthdays and they should always be celebrated. You should always feel celebrated and special on your birthday and with that, I asked Em out to lunch.

"I don't want to fight," she said. "Nor do I."

We were the only two patrons at the restaurant. She looked fragile. Thin. Tired. Spent. I don't know what I looked like but I felt how she looked.

She ordered prawns, and I ordered Steak. We ate. We laughed once. We stayed on longer than we needed to because we didn't want to leave each other. We were always drawn to each other. It's why she came back after leaving. She stayed in another room but she never left because I asked her not to and I'd hoped she wanted to stay. We just wanted to see each other, hear each other and if possible, touch each other. We were taking the hard road just to be with each other for a little longer.

That night I went to her room and we spoke. As I said goodnight, she pulled me closer for a hug. "I haven't been with her since that day" I was shocked she even raised the topic. I pulled away but she held me tight. "It ended that day." "Had I not caught you, would it have ended?" "I know it ended because you caught me and for the first time in my life, I feared losing you. You are my life and I would never want to be with anyone else. I gambled with our relationship and it opened my eyes"

"I watched you making love to her, it wasn't sex."

"I wasn't brutal with her, but I never loved her. You're wrong if you think I loved her. She left my life and I didn't even flinch. I'm afraid I'll die without you. I will do what it takes. Please be with me on this." I nodded in agreement. I led her back in our room, in our bed, in my heart, not that I ever removed her from my heart, truth be told, but we were terrified or at least I was, but I feared everything at this point. I was in complete survival mode, like trying to deal with getting the basics right. I regressed to a point of complete nothing.

It was different. She felt different. Of course she would, she was half her former self I justified. Making love to her was still so incredibly special and we had a connection that was deep and comfortable. Strangely, despite all the heartache, we still were able to be intimate. We slipped back into our friendship seamlessly but there were moments where I felt misplaced, disposed and no longer her confidant. We were separate for over six months and in that time we processed the separation in our own ways. I chose to become a hermit and she chose to reach out to her friends who helped her get through the breakup. She was closer to more people and they wanted to still be in her life. She was loyal to them and I realised their relationships had moved to a higher level. It would naturally do so if you open yourself up to them. There were profound friendships and I felt less important at times. My confidence had taken a knock and I felt as if I were no longer safe in a relationship that once meant everything to me. We had become different people and we were no longer as compatible. It was quite rare that we would be on the same page and sometimes we weren't even on the same book. There was a rift and it was growing bigger and we were feeling more fearful as we knew we were on the edge of a final breakup, but we held on and we tried and the grip was slipping until there was no hold anymore. I knew I was mostly to blame for the lack of progression of our recovery, because shamefully, I could not rid my head of the visuals, the sounds and the smells of the affair. I became more jealous, suspecting her of having more affairs. I failed, despite trying.

Chapter 43
Lets Let Go

History is a crazy thing. It creates ties that bind. In a break up or a separation or a divorce, those ties have to be broken, severed or simply ripped off. Any undoing is a hurtful process, no matter if it's ultimately a decision for the better. There is always that phase that brings the pain and anguish and torment. During this time I invited my angels into my life and begged them to stay close, to stay loving and to stay dear to me. I asked for signs constantly as I couldn't trust my own faculties anymore.

During a six-hour road trip after returning Dimitri to Durban as level three lockdown meant the re-opening of some tertiary institutions and the boys, Dimitri and Andrea could pick up on their Equestrian Sciences course, I spoke to my angels, alone in the car all the time.

The signs and messages were clear.

Angel number 555 is a message from your angels that it is time to let go of the 'old' that is no longer positively serving you. Trust that they will be replaced with 'better'. Release old doubts, fears and perceived obstacles, and if feeling any fears or confusion, ask for support and guidance from your angels.

Angel number 888 indicates that financial and material abundance is on its way into your life and may be suggesting that you will receive unexpected rewards for past good work.

Karma re-paid in kind. Angel number 888 tells you that your life purpose is fully supported by the universe.

Angel number 1111 signifies that an energetic gateway has opened up for you, and this will rapidly manifest your thoughts into reality. There is an opportunity opening up for you, and your thoughts are manifesting them into form at lightning speed. Angel number 1111 is similar to the bright light of a flashbulb.

If you see angel number 100, it means that your angels are reminding you of your inner wisdom and your ambition. Number 100 is also telling you that it may be the time for your spiritual journey, so it's important to get rid of all negativity and to change your way of thinking.

Now considering that if you type in any repeated number or number that you believe is a message from your angels, Google will spit out many interpretations of those numbers, so while driving and knowing this, I decided that I would read the first meaning my eye falls on as I travel steadily to my beautiful home. The fact that those four messages came to me when I was looking for answers in my loneliness, meant that the messages were absorbed, accepted and some made me feel relieved, and one brought back excitement again. An unfamiliar feeling which I cherished so I reread the message just to keep the feeling of elation a little longer.

Chapter 44
Our Home

She was spectacular. A double storey home that we both found online at the very same time and called each other immediately to confirm we'd found our perfect home. It was a beautiful experience. Me in Cape Town and she in Johannesburg searching desperately for our new home and then boom at exactly the same time, we found this stunner on page who even knows it's that far down the line. I think I've found our home, she smiled across the line. I think I have too, I giggled. She told me and I told her and we laughed at the coincidence of it all.

We had booked the movers and they were arriving on the 7th of December to load us up. The only missing detail was that we had no forwarding address yet. This was an uncomfortable situation to be in because we were seven in our family, including my mom who was visiting me from Cyprus at the time. We were seven and I needed to home us. Not having a home to buy was probably my fault more than anyone else. A real estate agent should never buy her own house. We're just too full of shit. The one prescription I had from the outset was, the house would have to have enough rooms to fit our large family because the kids needed their space, and quite frankly so did we. Truth be told, local agents just saw the potential commission and showed us all sorts of rubbish in the hopes that we would like something they showed us, anything they showed us, but none we had seen had actually even come close to it being a potential. Em eventually realised we'd get more done if she would look at homes and if she thought I would like one, we could go view it together on the weekend when I'd fly to Johannesburg.

We made an appointment to view the house we both spotted on page who even knows. We arrived and I was blown away by the view. The home was a double storey house, set in a stunning suburb, it was priced within our budget, and it was big enough to house our big, blended family. My mom, Em and I went through it with the agent and after showing us the property, inside and outside, we made an offer immediately.

That was ten years ago.

We both knew once our home sold, there was really no need to communicate anymore. We didn't share children to discuss future plans for them, we didn't share pets because I was going to take mine and she was going to take hers. We didn't share a business that needed buying the one partner out. We didn't share anything anymore.

The uncomfortable end was nearing and we were terrified.

Chapter 45
The Legal Work

Em recommended her close friend, Jane, who was a conveyancing attorney to process the sale of our home. Whenever Em recommended a friend, it always took me a second longer to respond, because I wondered if it was her "friend." I guessed Em knew what I was thinking from her eye contact and let the moment pass without comment.

Meeting at the attorneys to sign all the relevant paperwork was filled with both trepidation and anxiety. I put the feelings down to overcoming an old love that filled space in my heart for almost two decades Em was my best friend for over 20 years, so I rationalised that these feelings must be normal. I couldn't understand why we were being observed by the attorney until Jane asked us outright one day if we were certain that our relationship was not worth salvaging. Of course not, we both looked surprised at her blatant question. "Why do you ask?" continued Em, whereas I was quite satisfied to end the conversation right there and proceed with the legalities of selling our home.

"You are both quite tender and considerate of each other despite your claims that you want to end this. This is not the usual position my clients take when they're separating. I usually have to schedule them at different times, whereas you both are very accommodating of the other and quite frankly had I not known the intricacies of your past months, I would have said you're a solid couple with a deep love and understanding for each other." I kept my head down, scanning the page for places marked with x requiring either my initial and or full signature. I heard Em utter a sound of understanding, but I was not prepared to look up and participate in this conversation at all. I was done, she was done, we were done and it was all done. The fact that we were civil to each other was merely a reflection on upbringing and a mutual affection for each other as we sincerely did not want to hurt each other anymore. "I apologise if I've over-stepped," stated Jane in her official but friendly manner. I looked up, smiled and said.

"I think I'm done," not implying the irony as I pushed the papers to Em and referred her to the first page requiring her initial. She knew perfectly well where to sign, but I needed something to do to fill the awkwardness.

Jane walked us to our car explaining the legal work required for the transfer to take place and we were both content with the information as we nodded and accepted her details. There was complete trust in her and she made it perfectly evident that she was going to protect both in the transaction.

Chapter 46
The Recovery

"This is our last session Irene. You've done the work, since coming to me a year ago, on your own, very bravely. What are your thoughts?" asked Marina my therapist.

"I honestly don't know of a more confusing time in life than when your relationship ends and leaves you gutted. The devastation and push-pull and complexities of emotions and misconstrued words and the interventions and the cheapest commodity of mankind – opinions, drives one to madness. The mind development programmes start, self-affirmations, yoga, and meditation, business ideas in abundance and then total relapse. The fear sets in, the what if phase, the it's never going to work phase, and then sleep deprivation, because why not.

I have honestly been altered by her loss in my life. I take my part in the failed relationship. I see it. I know it. I face it. I sit with it. I heal it. When 2 souls are trying to find their way to each other, friends and family should not side with anyone. They should send love and light. The souls are hurting, despite what they may be showing and despite what you may be perceiving. Those souls are hurting. Their hearts are broken, because they both made a mess of everything. "You left, you should've called." "You hurt me so of course I left." The accusations will fly around in the beginning, the blame will be part of it for each other, but once the dust has settled, and everyone believes you've healed, but you're still gasping for air, whether you suffer from panic attacks or not, that's when the truth matters. For me it's simple, if 2 people love each other, and want to be together, they will find a way. There's no pride, or power in true love. Love is messy if you allow it to be, but in reality, it's very simple. You will be together if that's what you both want. There is always good in every situation, even in heartache, so I take the lessons, and forgive the rest. Onwards and upwards, well for now anyway, for today, because this healing process is a day by day journey."

Chapter 47
Hope

I have never loved anyone in my life as I have loved Em. I know it's cliché, but it's fact. I have loved and I have loved deeply. I still love the people I was with. I always will. Mario and Sarah have occupied a piece of my heart since the day I met them both. Mario crept into my heart little by little and to this day I am eternally grateful to him, for giving me the best gift I have ever received in my life – my children. They are ours and I cherish them. Sarah came into my life at my lowest point and she built me up to cope with life again. And Em, my dear Em, my beautiful Em, my soul mate. Sadhguru claims our soul does not have a mate, well I respectively challenge Sadhguru on that point.

When all the noise was removed from my head, and I simplified my thoughts and tried to settle them, I realised I wanted to grow old with Em. I wanted her care in my life, I wanted her tenderness in my life, I wanted her kindness in my life, I wanted her companionship in my life, I wanted her exquisite frame in my life, I wanted her soulful eyes staring at me in my life, I wanted her guidance in my life, I wanted her intellect in my life, I wanted her logic in my life and yes, dear God, I wanted her madness too. She came as a package and I wanted it all. I wanted her crazy, I wanted her moods, I wanted her vulnerability, I wanted her issues, I wanted her whole and I cherished her when she was by my side and for a little while, I forgot to be grateful for her, for her love and for the joy she brought to mine. I wanted her in my future and I was going to do whatever to make her see that I was more in love with her now than I had ever been before.

Therapy was necessary mostly because I couldn't get the affair out my head, and so I opted to move to Cyprus to start afresh after selling our home, and start the process of healing. I realised I could not be in the same city as Em, not even the same country, because we were always drawn to each other. I had heard she rented a new home, large enough to fit us, but she lived alone. I had heard she wasn't dating anyone. I found out the woman she had an affair with, was an attorney from another firm that they were considering to make a partner. She was renowned for using her sexuality to get what she wanted. The two never spoke after the day I caught them and she wasn't offered the partnership.

I called her literally a year after we sold our home and asked her to come to Cyprus for a visit. She obliged and within three weeks she was on a plane and flew into Larnaca Airport via Doha on Qatar Airways. Landing in Larnaca is always such a treat because you think you're going to land in the sea and then out of the blue the wheels find land.

When I saw her through the glass doors, I realised I was spot on with my plan. She came out and I walked towards her stepping faster with every movement, and so was she until we reached each other and held each other as if to catch up on all the time lost. She looked a sight and I held her face in my hands and said "you look so relaxed, so beautiful". She always took my breath away and today was no exception. I hugged and held her and smothered her in kisses and held her even more and as the tears rolled down my face, I took her hand and bag and directed her to the car. We drove to Paralimni in continuous conversation and she kept saying "You're beautiful Baby." "I have something to show you" I said giggling with excitement, "Me too" she winked. I missed her wink. I parked the car outside the building. The mediterranean across the road looked exquisite that day. "Where are we?" said the attorney. "You'll see." I opened her car door and let her take the building in. "Why does this look so familiar?" I gave her a moment. "Is this the building we fell in love with when we came on holiday in 2013?" "It is" I said excited to show her more. "IREMMA" "what does that mean?" she asked when she saw the name of the building. "It means calmly" I said, "That's divine, I love it." "I used IRE from my name and used EMMA from your name and called it IREMMA." As I looked away from her to unlock the big wooden door, she pulled me in and wrapped her arms around me. I turned around facing her and she was teary. "You make me so happy. I've missed you my love." I kissed her cheek and then her mouth and whispered "I love you Em." She kissed me and scolded me for taking too long to unlock the door. We laughed at our silliness and when I opened the door, her mouth gaped. "How? This is 'To Tavernaki'." "I know. When I got here I realised I loved the tavern so much. I knew I wanted to live by the beach and so I went searching for a site. I drove past this building as the owner was hammering a For Sale Board on the wall. I stopped and after a coke and a souvlaki, I made him an offer. He said he agreed because I reminded him of his wife who died due to Covid. He believes she sent me to him. I didn't have money, so I made arrangements to pay him with installments. He agreed and vola."

"Baby you're brilliant" she beamed. "But this is 'Tavernaki'." "Yes,I rented a container and shipped all the furniture, equipment and stock to Cyprus. Came three months later, by then I had given this building a little makeup." She laughed and said "I recall it was rundown, that's why I wasn't sure it was the same building." "I set it up as a legal business," she kept her eyes on me as I handed her the papers. She loved the law and immediately took the papers to ensure I was covered. "What's this?" she asked. "You know" I said smiling. "This says it's in my name and your name?" Her statement had more of a question ring to it. "It is my love. It's the only way I could think of showing you, I trust you." I went down on one knee and in true girl spirit, cried as the words came pouring out. "I want you to know that I give myself completely to you. I want to wake up every morning next to you and I want you to be the last thing I see when I close my eyes. I know I haven't always got it right and I'm sure I'm going to get plenty more wrong, but please know that with every day I'll do better or at least try to always do better. I promise you a life full of joy and sadness and kindness and madness but it will be a full life, a rich life and every night when we go to bed, I'll wrap my arms around you and make you feel safe because all I want to do is love you. Please, marry me, Em." I was crying so much getting the words out, I forgot to get the ring for my proposal. As I reached in my jeans for the ring Em went down on one knee, reached for a ring in her pocket and held it in her hands saying sincerely through sobs "You've always been the one, I'm sure of what I want, without compromise.

Please marry me Irene. We both reached out to each other, hugged, lost our balance, rolled over laughing and next thing I was on top of her. "What about your work?" "I came here to start a new life with you. It was never my intention to come for a holiday. They bought me out and so I am no longer a practicing attorney." she laughed.

"But you love it!" I shrieked.

"I love you so much more" she said. I placed the ring on her ring finger of her left hand as per South African tradition and she placed the ring on my ring finger on the right hand as per Greek tradition. We kissed and sealed it.

"What now?" she asked laughing and crying all at the same time.

"Now we get ready for opening night tonight." She looked at me with shock. "Tonight?"

"Correct!"

"Well you know what that means?" as she took me by the hand and led me to our office. "We need to…"

"Yes we do Agapi mou, yes we do."

The End